# *JAX*

BY

*Teresa Gabelman*

# ACKNOWLEDGEMENT

With this being a series I want each book to be different, yet I want to stay true to character without it being repetitive. I hope I have done that and continue to do that for as long as the Protectors Series continues. How long is that you ask? As long as you, the reader, desires.

The acknowledgement page, for me, is almost harder to write than the book. The reason being is that I never write alone. I may be the one writing the words, but so many others are right beside me. This is a joint venture that many contribute to.

So instead of naming I am going to say 'thank you' to every single person who has believed in me and my writing. At times when I want to pack up my computer as I did with this book…haha…you are there to pick me back up. I say you, because if you are reading this then you are beside me with everything I write. You are the reason I do what I do. I write for you because you believe in me.

There is a little surprise at the end of this book….please do not go to the end to see what it is because it will spoil it, it really will. DON'T DO IT!  You will see the respect I have for each and every single one of you. I do listen to my readers and I think you will see the proof of that at the end of Jax.

**A #2 Pencil & A Dream Can Take You Anywhere**
**Thank you for taking this journey beside me!**

The Protectors Series

JAX

# Chapter 1

Caroline didn't understand what she was doing there and had no clue where *there* was. She walked down a corridor, following a man in dark slacks with a white lab coat. The clicking of his hard-soled shoes on the tile floor echoed all around her. He kept looking at her over his shoulder without saying a word, as if making sure she still followed. She wanted to speak, but couldn't form any words. It was odd. Caroline always had words. Finally, he turned, heading into a room. She followed, but stopped in the doorway.

Her eyes roamed the all-tile room and stopped on the stainless-steel table positioned in the center of the room. A scale hung from the ceiling at the head of the table, which her eyes went back to. A body, covered with a stiff white sheet, lay motionless on the cold steel. The man just stood, arms hanging by his sides, as he watched her in an eerie silence.

"Who is that?" Caroline's voice finally forced its way out of her tight throat. When the man didn't answer, her gaze swung to his, narrowing angrily. "Who, dammit?"

His answer was a slow, smug half grin as he made a *tsking* sound in the back of his throat.

Taking a step toward the table, Caroline felt like she was walking in sludge. Her legs were heavy and it took great effort just raising them to move. Finally reaching the table, she grabbed the pristine crisp sheet in her fist, but didn't jerk it away. She was terrified, more terrified than she'd ever been in her life, to see who lay beneath. What was happening?

The man's *tsking* was driving her insane. He wouldn't stop, but she refused to look at him; instead, she stared at the body hidden under the sheet, willing herself to pull it away. She knew something wasn't right; it was all wrong. Feeling something touch her free hand, she looked down to see the little dead boy from her house, his pale face looking up at her with wide eyes. Slowly, he shook his head. Looking away from the boy, she spared a thought to his presence, but then he left her mind completely as she looked back at the body beneath the sheet. With a swift, strong pull, she yanked the sheet away, a scream freezing in her throat.

Lana, her twin, lay naked and pale on the cold steel table. Wide-open eyes, fixed in a horrified expression of pain and fear, stared back at her, her mouth slashed on each side making an exaggerated frown. Dried blood caked her neck, lower stomach, and the insides of her legs, indicating to Caroline that her sister had been violated violently.

"No!" Caroline's voice thawed in her throat, echoing in the sterile room. Her focus shot to the man who had finally stopped making the *tsking* noise, but before her gaze landed on him, she noticed more bodies covered with sheets filled the room, tables that weren't there before.

She shook uncontrollably as all feeling left her body and mind, leaving her numb. A rush of wind filled the room, pulling the sheets off, and exposing the bodies of the Warriors and their mates. Their expressions mirrored Lana's, but when her stare fell on Jax, his eyes were closed as if he were sleeping.

A sinister laugh burst free from the man who had led her to this nightmare, but her eyes never left Jax as she urged him to wake up. "Please." Her voice sounded so faraway, as if spoken from somewhere else. "Please, Jax." Caroline actually reached her hand out, but didn't take a step.

Suddenly, his eyelids popped open as his head snapped toward her. "Run!" Jax's voice filled her mind because his lips never moved, but his focused stare ordered her in a way only Jax's eyes could, and yet she stayed glued to the spot. She shook her head back and forth, refusing to leave him, leave any of them. "Run!" This time his mouth opened as the angry order filled the room.

Caroline jumped, her focus automatically going to the threat. The man watched her closely, his head tilted to the side with a crooked grin, and before she could react, he shifted into Jax's brother, Mika.

"Ah, sweet Caroline." Mika's voice was low, but sounded like he was singing under his breath. His head lowered as he looked up at her with a stare full of an evil she had never experienced before.

Transfixed by his stare, she wondered if he was

seriously singing "Sweet Caroline" by Neil Diamond to her, a song she'd despised with a passion growing up.

"You're crazy!" she whispered, glancing down to see a long gleaming blade in his hand tapping against his leg.

Lifting his head slightly, Mika ignored her whispered words, but continued the craziness. His singing stopped cold, the room becoming deathly silent as a grin spread across his face. He raised the knife to his own cheek, the blade edge tapping hard enough to break his skin. Blood trickled from the thin cuts. A steady stream of blood flowed the harder he tapped, ending at the corner of his cruel mouth. Slowly, he snaked out his tongue to swipe at the blood. "I've been wondering how you will taste, sweet Caroline."

Urgent, demanding shouts of "Run" filled the room. Each Warrior, their mates, and her sister had turned their heads to stare at her, urging her to flee. Caroline's feet finally moved as she backpedaled toward the door, her eyes scanning the horror before her as well as the smirking bastard who stalked her. Her back hit the cold doorframe and, with one last look at Jax, whose eyes never left her, she turned, propelling herself off the door to run down the hall. At first her footsteps were the only ones she heard echoing as her feet pounded the tile floor, but all too soon, another set of footsteps followed.

Rounding a corner, she saw a door with a red Exit

sign at the end of the hallway. The faster she ran, the faster the footsteps following her pounded. Fear kept her from turning around. Her focus was on the door. Something told her if she made it to the door, she would be safe. The faster she ran, the further away the door seemed to be. Tears blurred her vision but didn't slow her. At last, the door was within reach and, without slowing down, she slammed into it with her whole body as darkness engulfed her and she fell into the pitch-black of nothing.

******

Caroline sat straight up in her makeshift bed on the floor, her legs and arms flaying as a scream echoed in her empty house. Gulping for breath, she pulled herself to her knees searching for her phone. Swiping her hair, wet from sweat, from her face, she spotted her phone charging on the windowsill. Not even bothering to stand, because she wasn't sure her legs would hold her up, she crawled, grabbed it, and yanked the charger out of the wall.

"Please. Please." She whispered the plea as she juggled the phone in her shaking hands. Hitting Lana's number, she had to use both hands to hold it to her ear. Taking deep slow breaths to calm her heart rate, she listened to the ringing. With each ring, the knot in her stomach tightened. "Come on! Answer!"

When voice mail answered, she hung up and dialed again, praying with every breath she took. A movement caught her eye and she turned. The little boy stood in the shadows watching her. "How did you…?" She started to speak to the little boy, but Lana's phone clicked with Sid's greeting.

"Sid, where's Lana?" she cut him off.

"Are you okay, Caroline?" Sid's voice went from a friendly "Hello" to a concerned demand.

"I have to talk to Lana, now!" Caroline bit her lip, trying to keep control. Rationally, she knew that by talking to Sid it proved she'd had a terrible nightmare and that her sister was okay, but it wasn't good enough. She had to talk to her twin.

"Caroline, calm down," Sid commanded. She could tell he was instantly in Warrior mode.

"Do not tell me to calm down, Sid Sinclair," Caroline hissed, hating the anxiety in the pit of her stomach. "Is she there?"

"Yes, she's in the shower."

"Are you sure?" Caroline knew she was being irrational, but the dream had been so damn real, and being twins, she and Lana had a certain connection. Caroline knew her anxiety wouldn't leave her until she heard her sister's voice. "Put her on the damn phone, Sid."

"Lana." Sid's voice was distant, evidence he had pulled the phone away from his mouth. "It's Caroline, and she's upset wanting to talk to you."

"What's wrong, Caroline?" Urgency filled Lana's question. "Is it Mom or Dad, Jamie?"

"Oh, no, it's not..." Caroline sank back on her makeshift bed on the floor in relief. "It's just... I had a dream and needed to make sure you were okay. No big deal," she lied. "Listen, I'll talk to you later, and tell Sid sorry I was being an asshole."

Caroline hung up before Lana could respond and tossed her phone away from her. She then covered her eyes. Man, she had to get a grip. It was only a dream, yet it seemed so different. She quickly turned her head to look in the corner where the little boy had appeared earlier, but he was gone. Her phone ringing pulled her focus away. Sitting up, she saw Lana's picture flash on her phone. She grabbed her cell and hit Ignore. Knowing Lana would continue to call, she sent her a text saying she was okay and not to worry.

Looking down, she wasn't surprised to see her hands shaking and knew that if she sat there much longer thinking, she was going to lose it. "It was just a dream," she hissed to herself as she stood.

Walking to the kitchen, she went to start some coffee, but stopped. She needed to release her pent-up energy, which was weird since she'd just woken up. She was not a morning person and it took no less than one pot of strong 'knock you on your ass' coffee to get her going, but this morning was different.

Heading to her room, she grabbed a pair of sweats, a hoodie, and tied her hair in a sloppy ponytail. Searching around, Caroline found her tennis shoes and quickly put them on. Once finished, she headed for the door, but paused and looked at the coffee pot, knowing once she finished with a run she would want a cup. With a sigh, she hurried and started a pot before taking off out the door.

\*\*\*\*\*\*

Jax followed Sid and Lana down Caroline's dirt driveway. Blaze and Steve were behind him. They had set this time to come out and work on the roof, but after talking to Sid, the roof was the furthest thing from his mind. His patience was wearing thin. Dodging the ruts and puddles from the heavy rain they'd had the previous night, he maneuvered his motorcycle and passed Sid down the driveway.

He searched and missed nothing as he pulled his bike to a stop and hopped off. In five strides, he was on the front porch knocking on the door. When he heard nothing inside and Caroline didn't come to the door, he cursed, grabbed the knob, and opened the door.

"Caroline!" Jax called out, his gaze not missing the buckets and pots scattered throughout the house catching what rainwater the tarp they had placed on the roof didn't. It was pretty bad for a two-story house. He wondered how many damn buckets she had scattered upstairs. "Dammit," he hissed. He had wanted to stop by last night or at least call to make sure she was okay and the roof hadn't caved the rest of the way in, but Sloan had kept them so busy he hadn't had a minute.

"She here?" Lana ran inside with Sid close behind. "Where is she?"

Jax didn't answer, but walked to the coffeepot and felt it. "She's here somewhere." He cocked his head to listen, but couldn't pick up anything. It didn't look like a struggle had taken place, but it was hard to tell, with the house being in the chaos period of remodeling. "What did she say when she talked to you?" He turned toward Lana, his eyes darkening.

"She just said she had a dream. She seemed flustered, but that has happened before with our dreams." Lana frowned, but didn't add any more. "Caroline!" she called out.

Steve and Blaze had made their way inside. "What's going on?" Steve checked out the house, then walked over to peek down into the bucket before glancing up at the ceiling. "This place is definitely a stinker."

Everyone stopped to look at Steve. "What the fuck is a stinker?" Sid glared over at Steve.

"You know"—Steve spread his arms out, looking around the place—"a dump... a stinker."

"Where in the fuck do you come up with this shit?" Sid shook his head, still eyeing Steve as if he were some funky alien, but Steve just shrugged before walking around.

"Don't let Caroline hear you say that," Lana warned. "She won't invite you to dinner."

A piece of ceiling broke away, crashing in front of Steve. "And that would be a bad thing?" He stepped over the plaster. "You know, Blaze, you could do your 'hot to trot' thing and save Caroline and us a lot of misery by burning this baby to the ground."

"You have our permission to 'hot to trot' his ass," Sid told Blaze, nodding toward Steve.

"I don't 'hot to trot' anything. I set shit on fire." Blaze glared at Steve.

Steve snorted like Blaze was joking, but the swirling eyes glaring at him had Steve hurrying away from Blaze. Steve stopped next to Jax and touched the coffeepot that sat full on the coffeemaker. "She couldn't be far. Pot's hot."

"No shit." Jax growled, not in the mood for the usual Warrior comedy hour. Something wasn't right. The ringtone he knew was Caroline's started ringing. He stepped toward the bed she had made on the floor— it still pissed him off that she was sleeping on the floor—and found it resting there as if it had been tossed. He picked it up. "Who's Rachel?"

"One of the teachers at her school," Lana said, her voice worried. "She always takes her phone, Jax."

Jax headed for the door, putting Caroline's phone in his back pocket without answering it, and walked outside. His eyes searched for any clue, his head cocked to the side, trying his best to hear anything that would tell him where she was.

"Her purse and wallet are still here." Lana came out, followed by Sid, Blaze, and Steve.

Jax didn't say anything as he glanced toward her car. Where in the fuck was she? Dammit, this was exactly why he didn't let his feelings become involved with anyone. He hated to care about anything or anyone because bad things happened to those he cared for.

"Hey!" Steve snapped his fingers. "Can't you shift? I mean, I know you don't shift a lot, but couldn't you shift like Hunter and sniff her out?"

Jax had actually thought of that, but he wasn't an animal shifter. He could, but it took him forever to shift back and it wasn't pleasant. Yet, if he needed to do that to find her, he would. "I only shift into animal form if absolutely necessary," Jax replied, his eyes still scanning the area in hopes of spotting a clue. "It takes too long to shift back into human form."

"Ah, got ya," Steve replied with a nod, as if he knew exactly what Jax meant, but his next words proved he didn't know shit. "Guess it would be embarrassing having to hike your leg to pee."

Blaze probably saved Steve's life when he grabbed his neck and pulled him along beside him. "Steve, let's go check around back."

Sid actually chuckled, shaking his head. "And to think he's a Warrior. What the hell were we thinking?"

"I'm going to check the area around the house." Jax jogged down the steps. "Call me if she shows up or you find something."

"You want us to come?" Lana started to follow, but Sid stopped her.

"He can move faster on his own. And from what I got out of the very tight-lipped Jax Wheeler, he was one hell of an Indian tracker way back in the day." Sid wrapped his arm around her shaking shoulders. "She's fine, Lana. Jax will find her."

Damn straight he would find her, Jax thought as he took off. Sid was absolutely right. He could move faster on his own. Caroline was his main priority and he would find her, and it better be unharmed.

## Chapter 2

Caroline was glad she took the run. Refreshed, the morning air did her good as well as cleared her head. Slowing, she eased to a walk as she scanned the area and smiled. This was her land, or at least, she thought it was her land. She didn't know the exact landmarks, but it was close enough to her property, so as she stood there, she claimed it. A bird sang happily above her. She tipped her head back, closed her eyes, and just listened to the sounds of nature on *her* property.

Taking a deep breath, she stretched her arms over her head, then bent down and touched her toes. Placing her hands on her hips, she bent to one side and then the other. Slowly, she let out her breath, then decided to go down the trail she hadn't been on yet. She wanted to explore just a little longer.

Excited, she turned and started jogging. The trail was muddy from the heavy rains, but she didn't care. Nothing could ruin what was turning out to be a pretty good morning. After her nightmare, she'd definitely had doubts about the day ahead.

"What in the hell are you doing?"

Hearing Jax's voice behind her scared the hell out of her. In mid-jog, Caroline turned, her feet slipping in the mud, taking her to the edge of the trail, which emptied into a deep gully. The ground was so soggy it gave way underneath her and there was nothing but mud and rocks to claw at. She didn't even have time to scream, she was sliding so quickly with the sinking ground.

A hand grabbed hers, stopping her. She only had a second to look up into Jax's concerned face before more of the ground gave away underneath him.

\*\*\*\*\*\*

Sloan finally sat down behind his desk, his mood foul. His dark eyes searched his office, for what, he didn't know, because answers were not hidden in the empty walls that surrounded him. No, the answers were supposed to be coming from him, but he didn't have them and wondered if he ever really did.

He was a leader to many, and yet he felt less like the leader he once was and didn't even have a reason as to why. His phone dinged, indicating a text. His eyes followed the noise, but he made no move to pick it up. It would just be someone wanting something from him and, in all honesty, he just didn't have it in him at that moment to be the guy who everyone looked to for answers.

A knock on the door quickly followed the message and he ignored the pounding taps, just as he ignored his phone, but unfortunately, it didn't work. Duncan opened the door and walked in.

"Hey, didn't you hear me knocking?" Duncan asked, and took a seat in front of Sloan's desk.

"Yes," Sloan replied, his voice tinged with indifference. "I'm closed."

Duncan's eyebrows rose. "You okay, boss?"

Sloan's eyes met those of Duncan', a Warrior he had fought beside, even died beside, and he wondered when he'd grown so tired, so sick of the world he was forced to live in forever. Did he make a mistake so long ago? Should he have just died and been at peace when given the chance? The question had haunted him of late. Was he still the man who had taken the pledge to keep his race and humans safe in the face of any danger? Did he even know that man anymore? Did his Warriors see him slipping from being that man?

Before Sloan could open his mouth, the door opened again as Jared and Damon walked in. "Where's Sid and Jax?"

Duncan hadn't taken his eyes off Sloan, but Sloan finally looked away from his friend who had questions. Once again there were questions Sloan knew he wouldn't be able to answer.

"They went to finish fixing Caroline's roof," Duncan answered, looking away from Sloan.

"Heard the place was a money pit." Jared sat down next to Duncan, Damon taking his normal spot leaning against the wall.

Sloan didn't say a word. He had heard all about

Caroline's purchase, but didn't feel the need to put his two cents in. He had enough to worry about. There was something about Caroline that had attracted him to her, but he had squashed that real quick. It seemed she belonged to Jax Wheeler, whether Jax wanted to admit that or not. Maybe Jax needed a push before Sloan changed his mind about the little schoolteacher. Wouldn't that set the Warriors, who thought they knew him so well, on their asses?

When the room went silent, Sloan was pulled from his thoughts and found each Warrior staring at him. "What?"

"I hope to God I'm not going to have to pull my gun out on you again." Jared frowned, but his stare and harsh statement meant business.

"For fuck's sake." Sloan pushed back from his desk and stood. "It's me, you dumb ass, and if you pull out that gun and point it anywhere toward me, Slade will be surgically removing it from your ass."

"It's him." Damon nodded, a small smirk on his face.

"Well, with all the shit going down since Hunter decided to 'let the 'dog out' on the steps of City Hall, I'm on edge." Jared relaxed. "We got a call last night about a shifter who shifted to look like a woman's husband and they got their freak on. So the real husband came home to find himself in bed with his wife. It's freaky shit."

"Why in the hell are we getting calls like that?" Sloan growled, first glancing at Jared, then Duncan. "The human police can take care of those calls. Unless they are wolves, bears or anything in the animal kingdom and they are not part vampire, they have no power other than shifting."

"You know that, I know that, but the human police don't know that," Damon replied, with a disgusted sneer. "Once we got there, the police were standing behind their cars, guns out while the human male and shifter were fighting on the front lawn with the woman screaming and running around naked."

"And when we asked why they hadn't broken it up, they said because they didn't know who the shifter was and who the human was because they were identical." Duncan sighed with a shake of his head. "So they felt it was the VC Warrior's' job to take care of it since it was paranormal."

"Son of a—" Sloan stopped midsentence to rub the palms of his hands against his eyes.

"The shifters are running loose with no worries of facing the stiff penalties that their leaders put in place for coming out in public," Duncan added.

"Shifters gone wild. You know, I bet they will come out with a video of that pretty soon." Jared nodded with a snort, then frowned when Sloan dropped his hands from his eyes to glare at him.

What a fucking mess. "I need to meet up with all

pack leaders in the area," Sloan ordered. He knew that the wolf packs like the Lee County Wolves were in charge of shifters in their area. More would have to be trained to help keep things under control because his Warriors were spread thin as it was.

"Done," Duncan replied, opened his phone, and sent out a text.

"Although it was a pain in the ass call, we did find out some possible valuable information from the horny shifter." Jared gave a sly grin. "We felt, since we were bothered with this call, we might as well try to get something out of it, and we didn't even need to beat it out of him. He seemed happy to help."

Damon gave a rare chuckle. "I think he may have pissed himself, but no one touched him."

Sloan rolled his eyes and sat back down. Even these talks with his men wore him the hell out some days.

"Well, that was your fault." Jared eyed Damon. "You have a very scary side to you."

"I know," was all Damon said, no explanation, no denial, just plain acceptance.

"It seems that a new addition to the shifter community has been showing up regularly at one of the downtown hangouts," Duncan added, which Sloan was glad for, because honestly, he was about ready to… Shit, he didn't know what he was about ready to do. Loose his fucking mind, maybe.

"Mika, Jax's brother?" Sloan wondered for a brief second if things may start going their way, but refused to get his hopes up.

"That's what we are thinking and he fits the description." Jared cracked his knuckles, a predatory gleam in his golden eyes. "We just need bait."

"Jax won't go for that," Sloan replied with a shake of his head. Hell, he himself wouldn't go for it. No way would he put Caroline in danger.

"I'm not talking about Caroline." Jared grinned, then grabbed his phone from his pocket and shot out a text.

Damon was the first to understand who. "No way in the hell will Slade let her be bait for someone like Mika."

Jared just smiled. "My money's on Jilly." With a large grin, he pulled out a hundred-dollar bill.

Damon dug in his pocket then slammed a hundred on Sloan's desk, with Duncan doing the same thing. Everyone looked at Sloan. He wasn't about to take this bet. "What in the fuck did I do to deserve being a leader to a bunch of fucking assholes?" Sloan hissed, then sighed in one long breath. "No way in hell is this going to go over well."

******

"Absolutely not!" Slade glared at Sloan, who happened to see Damon and Duncan grinning from ear to ear.

"Absolutely not, what?" Jill walked into Sloan's office, holding her phone. "You needed to see me?"

This time Sloan looked at Jared, who now had a shit-eating grin on his face. "Yes, we have information that—"

"She's not doing it, so you might as well save your breath." Slade's tone was dangerously low as he stared at Sloan.

"You know what, Slade, I'm going to let this pass this once because this is your mate, but your mate has been sworn in as a VC Warrior and has obligations to—"

"Obligations to what?" Jill interrupted, then glared at Slade. "And I love you, but you don't speak for me. Nowhere in that ceremony did I agree that you speak for me."

"Damn. Guess she told you." Jared seemed to enjoy shooting that dig at Slade. Then he looked at Jill, cocking his eyebrow at her, knowing she was going to be all over it. "We have information where Mika might be hanging out."

"I'm in." Jill didn't wait for any more explanation. "I've been waiting for the chance to get my hands on that son of a bitch."

"Fuck!" Slade cursed, glaring down at Jill, who was scowling up at him.

Jared raised his hand, indicating with his fingers he was waiting for his money. "Pay up, bitches."

"I want my cut if you bet on me." She eyed Jared with a frown. "You make way too much money on me."

"No, Sid usually makes the money off you. But, I'll make sure you're taken care of, babe." Jared winked at her, then raised his hands at Slade's glare. "What?"

"This is too damn dangerous and you know it." Slade looked away from Jared to Sloan. "She is not going to be bait so we can catch our guy."

"Who says?" Jill jabbed him in the chest with her finger. "I thought we talked about this."

"You talked," Slade replied, grabbing her hand to stop her jabbing. "And I said we would go on a case-by-case basis."

"Oh, okay, Dad." Jill rolled her eyes. "You have no say over what I do."

"The fuck I don't." Slade's growl became hostile. "You are my—"

"Shut up!" Sloan's powerful voice shook the room,

quieting everyone. "Shut the fuck up and listen to me. I give the orders and I say she is bait. She knew the risks when she pledged to be a Warrior. Now get the fuck out of my office before you see a side of me you've never fucking seen before. I will let you know as soon as everything is set up."

"See what you did," Jill whispered in anger to Slade as they headed out of the room.

Slade stopped beside Jared and punched him in the stomach, hard. "Never call my mate babe again."

Jared bent over from the hit, but when he straightened, he had a huge grin. He grabbed the money, making a scene counting it. "Like taking candy from a baby."

Sloan rubbed his temples. He'd never realized vampires could get a headache, but his temples throbbed and he just wanted to get the fuck out. His eyes rose to see Damon, Duncan, and Jared all staring at him. With a sigh, he dropped his hands.

Jared put the money in his pocket. "Guess we're going over to help out on that roof and go over a plan. You coming?"

With a rare grin, Sloan stood. "Why the hell not." He needed to take his mind off shit and maybe some manual labor and fucking with Jax would be just what he needed.

## Chapter 3

It all happened so fast. One minute Jax had been searching the trails for Caroline, and the next, he was staring at her as if he'd never seen a more beautiful woman in his life. She'd been gazing up into a tree watching a bird. He now was holding her hand, feeling her slip as the ground gave away underneath them.

"I got you," he said, even as he felt their grip slip from the slick wet mud.

He knew almost before he felt the ground shift that he was going down with her. As carefully as he could, he pulled her up into his arms as he fell on his back, beginning their quick descent down the steep hill. He cradled her head against his chest as he watched the best he could for any dangers.

Using his feet, he did his best to slow their slide, but the mud was unforgiving. When he heard Caroline gasp out in pain, he held her tight with one arm and reached out his other, trying to grab anything that would at least slow them down. Finally, his hand caught a shabby-looking bush, but it was enough to stop them. As they jerked to a stop, he sat up, holding her close.

"Caroline, are you all right?" He looked down at her face pressed against his chest, her eyes closed tightly.

"Yeah, I'm fine," she replied, but he could tell by the paleness of her face she was lying.

"What's hurt?" Carefully, he forced her away from him. "Caroline?"

She eased up and felt her right side, then grimaced. "I think I hit a rock or something, but it's okay. It's nothing."

Jax frowned. Her lie was evident in the scent of her blood. The sweet, erotic smell had his fangs growing with pulsing need. Looking up the hill they'd slid down, then around trying to find the best way to get her out of there, he cursed. His head snapped back to her when she hissed in pain as she tried to move off him. He grabbed her hand and moved it away from her side before lifting her shirt up. A long, jagged cut from the waist of her pants to midway up her side bled freely.

"Nothing, huh?" He cocked his eyebrow, but still stared at the cut, then pulled her shirt down and replaced her hand on her side. "Keep some pressure on it. I don't think it's deep, but it's hard to tell and I don't want to touch it with my muddy hands."

Caroline nodded, doing as he said as her eyes took him in. "You're covered in mud." A hint of a smile lit her face.

"You should see you," Jax replied, stopping short of smiling himself. "Dammit, Caroline, what in the hell are you doing out here?"

The smile slipped from her face. "What do you mean, what am I doing out here?" she snapped. "What are *you* doing out here?"

"Looking for you," Jax snapped back, knowing he was being a total ass, and yet he couldn't stop himself. He was pissed and worried, more pissed since he had found her safe. Well, sort of safe. Son of a bitch, he about died again when he watched the ground give underneath her. "No one knew where you were."

"I knew where I was." Caroline slid away from him, but then slid further down the hill. He stopped the movement by grabbing her. She jerked away from him then grabbed on to the small bush to keep herself stable.

Jax grumbled deep in his chest, his eyes narrowing. "You left your house unlocked, left your phone, and I highly doubt you thought to bring your gun." When she didn't say anything, just knelt in the cold mud staring at him, he cursed. "I don't know how many times I have to tell you that my brother is out here somewhere just waiting for the perfect opportunity to strike. You are the easy target. He goes for the easy targets. At least make it a little more challenging for him."

Caroline's head snapped back in fear at the mention of Mika, but she didn't say a word.

"Has something happened?" Jax grasped her chin, not missing the fear in her eyes. "Dammit, Caroline, have you seen Mika? Has my sister contacted you?"

"You're a dick." Her words almost made him smile because she so didn't sound like the teacher he knew she was. "I went out for a run. I am a grown woman who can do things like that. I will not let the fear of your brother stop me from living my life. Yes, I should have brought my phone, but I didn't and it's really hard to run with a gun so I left it."

"Why, when I mentioned Mika, did fear color your eyes?" Jax probed, watching her closely.

"Color my eyes?" Caroline frowned, her head tilting as she stared at him.

"Yes," Jax replied, not understanding right away what she meant by repeating what he'd just said.

"You sounded so like a Native American." She searched his face, then shook her head. "Sorry, it's the teacher in me. And I don't know what you're talking about. I haven't seen or heard from either Mika or your sister. If I did, you would be the first to know, which is something *you* should know. I wouldn't keep that from you."

There was something about this woman that made it hard for him to remain mad or even irritated at her for very long, and that was rare. Everyone got on his nerves and he did hold grudges when people pissed him off, but had Caroline really pissed him off or was it the danger she'd put herself in that pissed him off?

"Are you profiling me?" Jax asked, his eyes searching her face.

"No." The smile started to come back, then she shrugged. "I guess I did stereotype you, maybe. I'm just fascinated...." She stopped talking, her face flushing beautifully.

That made two of them, he thought as he watched the different emotions play across her face. "Promise me you will be more careful." His voice was low, but the demand in his tone was evident.

"Okay." She nodded, then looked away.

Once again, Jax lightly grasped her chin to force her to look at him. "I'm serious, Caroline." He closed the distance between them by leaning toward her. "This isn't a game."

"I know." She leaned toward him, just inches away.

Jax tilted his head as his eyes stared into hers. He wanted nothing more than to kiss her right there, pull her underneath him and take her hard in the mud, in the middle of the wilderness. He knew it was his alpha drive urging him, but he fought it. This wasn't what one did in the twenty-first century and he needed to remember that. She was someone who deserved much more than having a quick mud fuck. Letting her go, he leaned away from her then stood, not missing the disappointment shading her face.

******

Caroline wanted to scream when Jax backed away from her. "Dammit," she hissed under her breath. He had to be the most irritating man she had ever met, and what shocked her most was that she wanted him more for it.

"What?" Jax had been looking up the hill, but when she hissed her curse, his gaze snapped back to her.

Shaking her head, she tried to stand. "Nothing," she lied. If she were a braver soul as well as a ho, she would just jump on him, rip his clothes off like she desperately wanted to, and make him pound her in the mud. She had to turn away from him because that thought turned her on, which made her moan deep in her throat.

He mumbled something under his own breath, but looked away from her and back up the hill. "I don't think we should try that way." He turned and reached out for her. "Come here."

Grasping his hand, she welcomed his strength as she slid in the mud moving closer to him. He bent and carefully picked her up. "Let me know if I hurt your side."

"I'm fine," she replied, being more than truthful. Being held in the safety of his arms definitely made her feel fine. Not knowing exactly what to do with her hands, she put one on his shoulder and the other on top of her own hand.

"Shit!" Jax cursed when he tried to take a step, but sank deep in the mud.

"I can walk." Caroline started to push away from him, knowing her added weight was making him sink deeper.

Jax didn't answer, but he grabbed her hips. "Wrap your legs around me." He positioned her where he wanted her. "You need to hold on tight. I'm going to jump."

She did as he said without question, putting her total trust in this man. Wrapping her legs and arms tightly around him, she sighed when he used one strong arm to hold her flush to his body.

"You ready?" His breath ruffled her hair.

She nodded and squeezed her eyes shut. She didn't close her eyes in fear; she knew he wouldn't let anything happen to her. Deep down, she knew it was so she could burn this memory in her mind forever. Being held like this, by Jax Wheeler, was something to be savored, and something she had daydreamed about.

"You can open your eyes now." Jax's voice broke through her thoughts.

Slowly, she opened them to find they were at the top of the hill, safely away from any danger of falling again. "Oh." She looked around, then at Jax. He slowly put her on her feet. Her sweatshirt rubbing against her cut made her groan.

"We need to get that cut cleaned." Jax frowned. "Can you walk?"

*Dammit, yes I can walk,* Caroline thought and yet, she totally wondered if she could lie so he would carry her back to the house. Knowing she wouldn't do that, she nodded. "Yes, I can walk." When Jax didn't say anything, Caroline started back down the trail.

"You're going the wrong way." Jax hadn't moved, but stood watching her.

"No, I'm..." Caroline looked around at her surroundings and frowned. "Obviously lost."

"Yes, you are." His tone sounded angry. "And that's exactly why you need your phone and firearm with you."

"Okay. Okay." Caroline slammed her hand on her hip, totally forgetting about the jagged cut on her side, and groaned. "Lesson learned. Now can we go, please? I'm cold, muddy, and I have to…"

"To what?" Jax eyed her when she stopped her sentence.

Caroline rolled her eyes at herself. She had to pee, but she'd be damned if she told him that. She almost did because her brain must be covered in mud like the rest of her body, making her a dimwit.

"Get some coffee." She huffed, angry with herself that she let this man get under her skin to the point she always felt tongue-tied and spoke without thinking. She never did that, ever... and did she actually call him a dick? This man had her doing and saying things that shocked her. "I'm cranky until I've had a pot."

"A pot, huh?" Jax moved to the side of the trail that fell away—or had the possibility of falling away—as Caroline moved next to him.

Caroline walked beside Jax as he led them out of the woods. A thought came to her. "What are you doing here?"

"Saving you," Jax replied without missing a beat.

Okay, she'd definitely set herself up for that. "Well I didn't need saving until you spoke out of the blue and scared me, which made me slip and then the ground gave way. I was perfectly fine before that."

"You know"—Jax held her arm to help her across a fallen log on the trail—"you suck at thank-yous. I saved you from falling through your roof and now this, but each time you blamed me."

"I place blame where blame is due, Mr. Wheeler." Caroline huffed, then felt bad. "And I did thank you, I think, when you saved me on the roof after you made me angry enough to stomp across the rotten wood. And I do thank you for stopping my descent down the hill when you caused me to slip by scaring the crap out of me."

Jax actually laughed. The sound was enough to make her stumble as tingles and goose bumps shimmered across her muddied skin and other parts that only he could bring alive.

"Yeah, you definitely suck at thank-yous." Jax didn't even look down at her, watching the trail in front of them, too focused on getting them out of the woods. "And I was getting ready, along with Blaze, Sid, and Steve, to come and work on the roof, but then Sid told me you called, frantic, so I rode out earlier with him and Lana. What had you so frantic, Caroline?"

Okay, now she felt like a total ass. He had been worried about her and all she could do was blame him for her own clumsiness. And no way was she going to tell him about her dream because, honestly, she didn't want him to disappear again, and knowing how he felt about his brother, he would do just that. In his own idea of making sure everyone was safe, he would walk away. Before she could apologize or explain anything, her house came into view and Lana, followed by Sid, was running toward them.

"Where in the hell have you been?" Lana reached her, her eyes roaming first down Caroline's body and then Jax's. "And what exactly have you been doing?"

Sid also checked them both out, a huge grin spreading across his handsome face. "About time, buddy." He elbowed Jax with a wink.

"Shut the fuck up, Sid," Jax growled, then looked at Lana. "She fell and has a cut on her side, that's it. We need something to clean the wound."

"Are you okay?" Lana's knowing grin slipped into a worried frown.

"I'm fine." Caroline started walking toward the house. Jax didn't have to sound so disgusted at Sid and Lana's misconception of why they were muddy. "But no one will be fine if I don't get a cup of coffee." She pushed past Sid who still wore a grin, mixed with concern.

Steve and Blaze stood by the side of the house, both looking at her. "So," Steve began and just the look on his face clued Caroline in on a joke coming on. She didn't know Steve well, but knew him well enough to know she didn't want to hear what he was about to say. Her mood had soured greatly.

She walked right up to Steve and stopped. "If you're not going to say, 'Caroline, you have a strong steaming cup of coffee sitting inside waiting for you,' I highly suggest you say nothing at all, Steve."

Clamping his mouth shut, Steve nodded. As Caroline continued on her way, he cursed. "Shit!"

"You unplugged the coffeepot, didn't you?" Blaze pinched the bridge of his nose when Steve didn't answer, but took off, passing Caroline to run into the house.

## Chapter 4

The hammering, cursing, and noise that came along with remodeling was killing her already pounding head, but the sounds were welcome because it meant soon, she wouldn't have to worry about the rain anymore.

Lana had left to grab some lunch, but Sid had stayed to help with the roof. After her shower, Caroline had cleaned her wound, which wasn't deep at all, and then grabbed her first cup of coffee. It was already late afternoon, but she didn't care. She needed her coffee. Steve had panicked because he'd unplugged it, not realizing her absolute need for it. He was still apologizing.

Picking up another pot full of rainwater, she headed out on the front porch to dump it. She had five more to go before all the pots were emptied, and that was just downstairs. She had more upstairs to get to. They had helped, but not much. Every time she'd thought she had it, another stream of rainwater broke free, so she would have to run upstairs and try to find where it was coming from. She just hoped she wouldn't have to replace all the upstairs' flooring. Why hadn't it rained the day she looked at the house? Maybe... nope, she would have still bought it.

Hearing her ringtone, she stopped pouring the water and listened. She hadn't seen her phone since that morning, and it sounded like it was coming from above her. Jax appeared in front of her as he jumped from the roof.

"Is that my phone?" She frowned, reaching for it, but he held it, looking at the screen. "Why do you have my phone?"

"Why is Rod calling you?" Jax's eyes shot up to hers. "I told that son of a bitch—" He growled out the words, but stopped before saying anything more.

"Told him what?" Caroline reached again for her phone.

"To stay the fuck away from you," he replied, not holding back his feelings whatsoever.

"Oh, ah..." That set her back a second. "I haven't answered. I would block his number, but I don't know how and haven't had a chance to figure it out so I just hit Ignore." After she spoke, she wondered why she felt the need to explain anything to Jax, but his demanding voice made her do things she normally wouldn't do.

"What's your passcode?" When she didn't answer, Jax's frown deepened.

Heat moved from her neck straight to her cheeks. "Here, I'll put it in."

Jax actually chuckled, handing her the phone. "Afraid I'll know all your secrets?"

Oh, wasn't that a loaded question that no way in hell she would ever answer. The fact was, she just got this phone because she'd dropped her other one in a damn bucket of water from her leaking roof. She was able to keep her old phone number, but she had to input a new password. Her cheeks burned as she punched in 5299, unlocking her phone. She didn't want him to figure out that 5299 had no other relationship to her other than it spelled out JAXX with two Xs. God, she was such a freaking loser, and at that moment she hated herself for crushing on this sexy Warrior standing in front of her who obviously didn't find her attractive enough to take full advantage of her in the mud, and no, that wasn't the lowest point in her thought process. That had come when she'd showered. She had fantasized about him wiping off every bit of mud from her with his bare hands.

"There." She handed him the silenced phone. She couldn't even look him in the eye.

"You have over fifty missed calls from the bastard." It was not a question, but an angry observation. Jax tapped on her phone in total concentration, then looked up and handed it back. "Blocked."

"Thanks." She stuck it in her back pocket, grabbed the pot, dumped the rest of the water out, and turned, all without looking at him.

"Caroline." His voice stopped her, actually made her cringe. When she didn't turn around or say anything at all, he walked up on the porch, standing directly in front of her. "How's your side?"

"Fine." For an educated woman, she sure was limited with her vocabulary when it came to talking to Jax Wheeler. She didn't want to look up at him because she was afraid he would be able to actually see every secret she had, and they all involved him. In avoidance, she stared at his chest, but that wasn't very safe either. Her eyes moved lower, but then jerked quickly to his arm. Holy hell, there wasn't anywhere safe to put her eyes on this man. Quickly, Caroline gave a short nod and stepped around him. "Good," she added, before practically running into the house.

Once inside, she took a deep breath and set the pot down, then stared at the other full pots. Well, they were going to have to stay there full, because no way in hell was she going to go back out there and face Jax again, not after her one-word replies, as if she didn't truly understand the English language.

Grabbing her phone out of her back pocket, she rubbed her fingers against the screen, thinking of Jax using her phone. "Stop it!" Caroline scolded herself. "Just stop!"

Entering the passcode on her phone, Caroline knew as soon as possible, she was going to change it. It was a little-girl move, using Jax's name, and it wasn't cute. It was dumb and just plain sad if she were being honest. Maybe it was time she moved on and stopped this silly infatuation she had with the Warrior.

Her stomach pitched with the thought of not seeing Jax anymore, but sometimes it was important to be honest with yourself and maybe she was at that point. He'd had plenty of opportunities to take it further, but hadn't. She knew he had to know she was interested, but he hadn't taken advantage. Caroline actually laughed at where her thoughts were going. She was upset and giving up because a man hadn't taken advantage of her. Boy, wouldn't the women's rights movement be upset with her.

Caroline snorted at herself, but frowned when she checked the missed calls. Jax wasn't exaggerating; she did have fifty missed calls from Rod, and one from her friend and fellow teacher, Rachel. She had hoped Rod would disappear, but it didn't look like that was going to happen. What confused her was Jax didn't appear happy about it. He'd actually looked enraged before he hid his anger behind the calm he portrayed so well. The ass.

\*\*\*\*\*\*

Jax went back to the roof, but had actually been one step away from hopping on his bike to find that son of a bitch. Fifty fucking missed calls. He guessed Rod hadn't learned his lesson, the little prick. He'd forgotten he had put her phone in his back pocket until it had started ringing, and he was glad he had. He was sure Caroline wouldn't have told him that asshole was bothering her. Picking up the hammer, Jax grabbed a board and nails. With more force than necessary, he pounded them in place.

"Dude, we're trying to fix the roof, not destroy it. Who called Caroline's phone?" Sid asked as he sat on a beam. When Jax just looked up at him without saying a word, Sid rubbed his chin. "I know it was somebody that pissed you off, because, not that you aren't pleasant to be around, but when you checked and hopped off this roof, I actually feared for someone's life."

"Her ex is calling her again," Jax finally said, his mood becoming darker. One thing that could send him into a rage was when people took his threats lightly, and it seemed like this stupid fuck was one of those people.

"Muscle head?" Sid's eyes popped open in shock. "Damn, he either has a big set of balls or he is the dumbest son of a bitch breathing."

"He won't have any balls when I'm finished with him." Jax picked the hammer back up, grabbed another board, and pounded fiercely.

"Can I watch?" Sid replied, then quickly added, when Jax looked at him from under lowered lashes, "Not cutting his balls off, but if you're a man of your word, which I'm sure you are, you did threaten him with a scalping."

One eyebrow cocked as Jax looked away to begin hammering again.

"I mean seriously, man." Sid looked thoughtful. "I always wondered how in the hell Indians did that to people with so much precision. And I bet you're damn good at it."

"I am," Jax agreed with a sinister grin. "And you are a sick son of a bitch."

"Yes, yes I am." Sid nodded in agreement before turning to finish what he was working on. "But I've much respect for you."

Jax didn't respond, he just kept his focus on his work. His mind, however, kept going to Caroline. She was definitely a puzzle and in all honesty, he hated puzzles, but she was one he wanted to slowly put together. He knew he could have had her in the mud today; she'd been primed and ready. She deserved more, much more, than a quick fuck in the mud by a Warrior who had nothing to his name other than a brother who wanted to shower terror down on anyone he showed any fondness for. He had learned that the hard way.

"Hey, what's everybody doing here?" Steve, who was doing his best to look like he was actually busy and doing something, pointed with his hammer. "Please tell me they're here to help. Roofing sucks monkey nuts and if they help, we can get done so much faster. And how in the fuck did Adam and Jill get out of this when I'm up here sweating balls? They better be here now to do some damn work."

"I doubt they're here to help." Sid got up and headed toward the end of the roof, ignoring Steve's outburst. "Sloan doesn't do roofs. Something's up."

Jax remained where he was, but frowned when he spotted Sloan walking up to Caroline, who had come out to greet everyone. His frown deepened when she smiled up at Sloan, her face blushing beautifully. Sloan glanced up, his eyes meeting Jax's, a slow smile tipping the corner of one side of his mouth before his focus went back to Caroline. Jax gripped the hammer tighter. Any tighter, and the wooden handle would explode within his grip.

"So, what do you think?" Caroline was asking Sloan. Jax could hear everything perfectly and waited for Sloan to reply.

"You did real good, Caroline." Sloan's voice sounded closer, making Jax glance their way. They were walking toward the back of the property while everyone else stood talking in the front. "It's a lot of work, but I have no doubt you will make this place your own in no time."

Jax snorted and growled at the same time.

"Thank you." Caroline had stopped to shine one of her beautiful smiles back at him. "Everyone who has seen it so far has told me that I've made a big mistake and to burn it down, but I see something different. This is already home to me."

Everyone? Jax looked away with an angry sneer. He didn't see anyone else up on the roof at the moment working their ass off to help her make this place livable. And he'd never once told her to burn the place to the ground, though he may have thought it.

He raised the hammer to angrily slam it down on the nail he hadn't finished hammering. Sloan was lying his ass off.

"I'll be more than happy to stop by and help out where I can." Sloan's reply and tone of voice hit Jax.

Instant rage radiated throughout Jax's body as the hammer missed the nail and found his thumb. He may be a tough vampire who had been shot, stabbed, hell, you name it, but smashing one's thumb with a hammer hurt like a bitch.

"Motherfucker!" Jax dropped the hammer and grabbed his thumb.

"Jax!" Caroline called, heading his way. "Are you okay?"

"I'm fine." he growled, then cursed when the pain throbbed all the way up his arm. Fuck, that hurt.

"Get down here and let me see it," Caroline called up.

"I'm fine," Jax repeated, his eyes going from Caroline, who glared up at him with her hands on her hips, to Sloan, who couldn't wipe the grin off his face.

"Come down here right now, Jax Wheeler, and let me see or I'm coming up there," Caroline demanded. If he weren't so pissed and in pain, he'd smile at her trying to order him around. Then again, he didn't want her climbing the unsteady ladder she had set up on the side of the house, and he sure as hell didn't want her walking around on the roof that was nowhere close to being safe.

With a curse, he stood and leaped to the ground, landing light-footed next to her. She grabbed his hand carefully to look at it. It looked like a busted thumb with blood leaking from beneath the nail.

"You need to be more careful." She turned his hand over, palm up, with a frown, to check it that way. "I'll go get a Band-Aid for it."

Jax stared down at the top of her head as something deep inside him cracked. It had been so long since anyone had cared for his well-being and it felt damn good. It also scared the hell out of him, so he forced the crack closed. He couldn't afford to let anyone care. It wasn't worth the risk and he wouldn't let anything happen to this woman because she showed him any kind of care, friendship, or— He cut those thoughts off, pulling his hand away.

"It's already starting to heal," he replied, with a gruffness that made her frown up at him. "I'm fine."

"I'm putting a Band-Aid on it whether you want it or not." Caroline narrowed her eyes at him. "If you're helping me and get hurt, I'm taking care of it whether you like it or not, so get over it, Warrior."

Before Jax could say another word, she walked past him to go get the Band-Aid. He felt that crack creaking open again and cursed. Feeling Sloan staring at him, his head snapped his way. "What?" he growled, wanting nothing more than to punch the smug look off Sloan's face.

Sloan cocked an eyebrow, but didn't respond because Caroline was coming back at a fast clip.

"Let me see." Her voice was firm, daring him to tell her no.

When he raised his hand, she gripped it carefully and gently put some antibiotic cream on it. "I don't get infections, Caroline." He was going to have to seal that fucking crack closed because at that moment, he wanted nothing more than to drag her into his arms and kiss her senseless for caring about his fucking thumb. "I'm a vampire."

"I know exactly what you are and it won't hurt anything, so shut up and let me take care of this." Her focus was on bandaging him without causing pain, and yet she was causing him pain beyond anything she or he could ever imagine. Caring for him could mean the end of her life and that was something he couldn't overlook, no matter how badly he wanted to.

## Chapter 5

After bandaging Jax's thumb, Caroline went back inside to help Lana set out the food she'd returned with.

"You planning on feeding an army?" Caroline opened the bread, setting it next to the platters of lunch meat on the table.

"Yes." Lana laughed, nodding. "You've never seen those Warriors eat before. I seriously doubt I bought enough."

They continued to work in silence, except for the radio playing in the background. She loved the oldies station and her students always made fun of her. During study times in her class, she would let them play the radio on one condition: at least once during the week, they would listen to her favorite station. They moaned and groaned about it, made fun of most of the songs and yet, they respected her because she understood them and allowed them to be who they were: high school students. Kids who loved rock, rap, and something in between—she still hadn't figured out what that exactly was yet. She let them be individuals.

"So, what was that call about this morning?" Lana asked without looking at her, busy setting out drinks, plates and utensils.

"Just me being dumb." Caroline kept her gaze on the

task, knowing if she looked at her sister, Lana would call her on the lie she was spouting.

"You might be able to fool Sid, but not me." Lana stopped what she was doing to stare at Caroline. "Spill it or I'll have the Warriors interrogate you."

"Seriously, Lana." Caroline rolled her eyes. "It was just a weird dream and I wasn't fully awake when I called. It's nothing."

Caroline knew for a fact if she told Lana the details of her dream, she would tell Sid, who in turn would tell Jax, and she didn't want to tell Jax. Maybe she should, but in all honesty, she was afraid he would leave, disappear in some heroic man thing to keep her safe. He was so strange about his brother, and the last thing she wanted was for him to vanish from her life because he felt it would keep her safer.

"Our dreams are different, Caroline, and you know it." Lana eyed her thoughtfully, then looked behind her. "If the threat of the Warriors interrogating you doesn't work, then I'll just have to ask the little boy who keeps peeking around the corner."

*Dammit!* Caroline turned to see the dead little boy, who she still didn't know anything about, staring at her with his sad eyes. Knowing her sister couldn't see her, she mouthed "'no'" to him. When he gave a slight nod before disappearing, she sighed with relief. Turning back to her sister, she frowned.

"He doesn't know anything because there isn't

anything to know, and you just scared him." Caroline decided not looking at Lana was best because her sister always knew when she was lying. The boy did know something, and Caroline needed to figure out what that something was.

"Bullshit." Lana pointed her fork, with an olive speared on the end, at her.

"Oh, thank God." Steve walked in the door and Caroline wanted to hug him. Her sister was tough and Caroline had a hell of a time lying to her; she always got caught. "I was about to perish out there, slaving away on that roof."

"You nailed one board." Blaze shook his head as he passed Steve.

"Yes, I did, and I did an awesome job if I do say so myself." Steve huffed with pride. "I want to make sure that it's perfect for Caroline. Plus, it's almost dinner time if my stomach is correct, which it always is. I totally missed lunch."

Caroline laughed at Steve when he batted his eyes and gave her a sappy grin. "Eat." She handed him a plate.

Soon Caroline's house was full of Warriors, and Lana was right: she hadn't bought enough food. Caroline didn't even get a sandwich, but she wasn't really hungry anyway. For a little while, she had forgotten about the dream, but with Lana bringing it up, it was at the forefront of her mind, making her jumpy. Her eyes kept going to Jax, who stood alone. She noticed he hadn't eaten anything either.

If anyone had told her a year ago she would have a group of VC Warriors helping her rehab her home, she would have laughed and called them crazy. But because of Lana and Sid, they were a part of her family now and she couldn't be happier.

"We need to fill in Jax, Steve, Blaze, and Sid," Sloan announced, his voice filled with authority.

"Fill us in on what? We finally going to get to do something more exciting than fix a roof?" Steve was in the middle of making himself another sandwich. His eyes popped up to Caroline's. "Not that I mind fixing your roof."

"You nailed one fucking board," Blaze added again with a shake of his head. "You haven't fixed shit."

"Hey, stop the hate." Steve pointed his sandwich at Blaze. "Perfection takes time."

"No, dumb asses take time." Blaze glared at the sandwich Steve pointed at him and it started to smoke.

Steve looked away from Blaze to his smoking sandwich. "Dude, so not cool." Steve stared at his sandwich, then shrugged, taking a big bite. "Then again, toasted ham and cheese is pretty amazing."

Caroline laughed, watching in awe. "I still can't

believe you have the power to do that." She glanced at Blaze who had a half smirk on his face, watching Steve demolish the rest of the sandwich.

"Yeah, he's a walking, talking toaster oven," Steve answered for him before grabbing a handful of chips and heading away from Blaze quickly.

"Are you done?" Sloan glared at Steve, who had just shoved a whole handful of potato chips in his mouth.

Steve's eyes widened and he opened his mouth to speak, but he might as well have been trying to whistle with a mouthful of crackers, because all that came out was crumbs of potato chips. He held up a finger as he chewed quickly, but Sloan's growl had him backing up behind Lana.

"Jared and Duncan went on a call. I'll spare you the details," Sloan began.

"Ah, damn, Sloan, the details were the best part of the call." Jared frowned. "A horny shifter—"

"I definitely want to hear about the details." Sid raised his hand. "All in favor of hearing about the horny shifter details, raise your hand."

Caroline just stood back watching the Warriors in action, and she had to say it was entertaining. Not only were they the fiercest men she had ever met, but the funniest. She watched as Steve raised his hand. Adam and Jill just laughed as Damon, Slade, and Duncan all wore matching serious faces. And Jax was watching her, his face emotionless.

"Enough!" Sloan shouted, making her jump. "We may have a lead on Mika."

Caroline's eyes shot to Jax, whose face was no longer emotionless. He had the look of the intense Warrior she knew lay close to the surface of the man she knew so little about. Her eyes moved from him to the rest of the Warriors. The change in their demeanors was impressive. No longer were they in a joking mood. It was as if they were ready for war.

"Where?" Jax's voice cut through the room with a tenseness that matched the stern look on his handsome face.

"There's a club downtown, a shifter hangout called the Venue," Sloan began, eyeing Jax. "And before you go running off, we already have a plan set up."

"Has he been seen there?" Jax didn't back down from Sloan's warning.

"The horny shifter gave a positive ID of your brother," Jared replied. "Seems like Mika has become comfortable and doesn't think he has to hide his identity."

"He's making himself known for a reason," Jax warned, his eyes going to each Warrior. "Believe me when I say everything he does is for a reason, his end goal, and he does have an end goal. If you don't start realizing how smart and evil my brother is, we lose. And what we lose is what we hold most dear to us."

Caroline actually shivered, images of her dream playing across her mind. Jax wouldn't even look at her, but as hard as she tried, her eyes wouldn't leave him.

"He can fucking try." Sid growled the words, pulling Lana close to him.

"Yeah, well that's not all," Jared added, glancing at Sloan then Jax. "Seems he's recruiting a bunch of shifters to start a council of their own."

"I have already contacted some of the local shifter leaders to let them know. They're obviously not happy, but we can't wait for them to do something about it. If Jax feels that he's a threat to us and those around us, we need to stop him now," Sloan replied, his eyes narrowed.

"Yeah, well, there's only one council," Sid sneered in anger. "And we're fucking it. So what's the plan to stop this bastard?"

"We're going to draw him out by sending Jill in," Sloan began.

Jax immediately shook his head. "And you will be playing right into his hands. That's exactly what he wants." Jax walked toward Sloan. "He's showing himself to bring us out on his terms. If we send in

Jill, he will know that we're there for him."

Sloan thought for a minute. "Okay, then what do you suggest?"

"I can do it," Caroline blurted, wondering if she had totally lost her mind, but to her it made sense.

"No!" many male voices rang out in unison.

"If any of you are seen anywhere near the place, he will know." Caroline shrugged, as if she didn't care whether they listened to her or not. She wanted Mika caught almost as badly as the rest of them, if not even more so because she strongly felt that was exactly why Jax hadn't made a definite move for her.

"Not happening," Jax replied, his tone final.

"I would be safe." Caroline didn't back down. "My date would make sure of it."

"And who the fuck would that be?" Jax took a step toward her, his voice going from final to deadly.

"Caroline, this is Warrior business." Lana tried to defuse the situation. "I don't think bringing up—"

Caroline didn't even look at Lana, but stared at Jax. "You."

"Uh, Caroline." Steve broke in with an exaggerated shake of his head. "I think you need to leave the

Warrior stuff to us because I think Mika would know his own brother."

Caroline broke eye contact with Jax and moved her eyes to Steve with a cocked eyebrow. "Wow, it takes a Warrior to figure that out?" She turned her attention back to Jax. "And he wouldn't know it was Jax if Jax wasn't Jax."

"Not a bad idea." Damon gave her an impressed nod.

"How could Jax not be Jax?" Steve snorted.

Everyone ignored Steve, who looked totally confused.

"It won't work." Jax shook his head. "Mika would know."

"I think you give your brother too much power," Caroline whispered, but knew he heard her if the glare he sent her way was any indication.

"Well, we can't let this opportunity pass. It has to be checked out, so it's either Jill or Caroline. I wasn't for letting Caroline anywhere near the situation, but she actually has a pretty good idea, and your brother doesn't really know her as he does Jill. Seeing Jill walk in without Slade would be a dead giveaway. And if you shift, you'll be there to keep her safe," Sloan added, as Jax continued to glare at Caroline. "So what's it going to be, Jax? You know your brother better than anyone."

"Ahhhh!" Steve said loudly with a snap of his fingers. "I get it now." Adam smacked him on the back of the head.

"When are we wanting to do this?" Jax turned away from Caroline.

"The quicker the better. We don't want him to move on, if it actually is him," Sloan said, then looked around at every Warrior. They nodded in agreement. "Tomorrow night. It's Saturday and will be busy."

Jax didn't say a word as he slammed out of the house. In the next minute, the sound of pounding from the roof echoed through the house. Soon, all the Warriors left until only Caroline, Jill, and Lana remained.

"Guess you get to play Warrior." Jill grinned at her.

"Hope you're ready for this, Caroline," Lana replied, eyeing her. "This isn't a game."

"No shit, Lana," Caroline hissed at her sister, then glanced up at the roof. She hoped she was ready also, since it was her stupid idea.

Caroline began cleaning up. Grabbing the empty platter, she headed for the sink. With only the sounds of hammering in the now quiet house, the radio played clearly in the background. The platter dropped from her hands, shattering across the floor, as the opening lyrics to "Sweet Caroline" filled her with terror.

# Chapter 6

Jax saw red as he hammered furiously, angry enough to crack the hammer right off the wooden handle. "Shit!" He tossed it off the roof. He'd heard Caroline's whispered remark about him giving Mika too much power. She didn't understand, none of them understood.

"Hey, man, relax." Sid came up behind him, taking a place on the roof. Soon, the roof was full of Warriors. "We got this, and Caroline's idea is pretty fucking smart. We can hit him and he won't even know it's coming."

Jax didn't say anything. He didn't shift often, hated shifting if he were being honest. But what bothered him most was putting Caroline in danger, actually *more* danger. Mika may not know the full extent of her relationship with him, but if their plan didn't work, then Caroline's involvement would be fully exposed. He wasn't sure he wanted to chance that. The risk was too great. Hell, he was already putting her and everyone else around him in danger just by being a part of their lives. Mika needed to die. He should have killed him when he had the chance, but that was the past. He hadn't, and he was now paying for that moment of mercy he'd given his brother.

"She'll be fine, man," Slade added as he carried a stack of wood, careful of where he stepped.

"And I'm sure you were all for Jill going in there knowing she could run into Mika again?" Jax glared up at Slade.

"She's my mate," Slade replied, his eyes narrowing. "Anytime my mate and danger are mentioned in the same breath, I'm not happy. What's your excuse?"

"Ehhh, ahhhh." Steve cringed, looking between Slade and Jax. "So, ah, Jax, who do you think you'll shift into? Man, how cool would that be? I'd shift into one of the One Direction dudes. All the women love them."

"One Direction?" Adam glanced at Steve. "Who in the fuck is that?"

"Are you kidding me?" Steve looked at him like he was a moron. "You don't know who One Direction is?"

"Do I look like I'm kidding?" Adam gave him a blank stare.

"It's the boy band that fills arenas with screaming women." Steve sighed. "Seriously, to have a gig like that. How do they get so lucky?"

"You want to throw him off the roof or you want me to do it?" Blaze glared at Steve, but asked Adam.

Sloan walked over, ignoring Steve, and started ripping off old wood as if he knew what he was doing. He checked over the side of the house, and then threw it down. "We'll have the place covered, Jax, and you'll be right there with her." Sloan took the new piece of wood that Damon handed him. "I don't like the idea any better than you do. Letting a female who's not Warrior status be involved in an operation is not ideal, but it's a pretty solid cover."

"If I have any feeling of unease, I'm getting her out of there. To hell with the plan," Jax stated, his voice indicating his statement was not up for debate.

"I wouldn't expect you to do anything else," Sloan replied, tossing Jax another hammer. "Now, let's get this fucking roof done before it rains again."

The Warriors worked in silence until a loud sound of breaking glass blasted from underneath them. Jax was the first off the roof. Slamming inside, he spotted Lana and Jill staring at Caroline, who stood in the middle of broken glass. She was staring at the radio, her face pale.

Lana grabbed his arm, stopping him with a shake of her head. She also stared at the radio. Jax stopped, but kept a close eye on Caroline surrounded by the shards of glass. Everyone had filed into the house, but no one said a word as Lana closed the distance to her sister.

"Why is the little boy pointing to the radio, Caroline?" Lana looked from Caroline back to the radio. Sid quietly came closer, but stopped when Lana raised her hand.

"I don't know," Caroline whispered, her voice quivering, as did her body.

"I know you're lying," Lana hissed harshly, but kept her voice low. "You hate this song, I know, but you look terrified and that little boy is trying to tell you something."

"What the fuck is going on?" Jax ignored Lana's outstretched hand as he moved forward, the glass crunching under his boots.

"Dammit." Lana sighed. "You scared him."

"Jax didn't scare him." Caroline still stared that way.

Jax had had about enough. He grabbed Caroline, gently turning her toward him. The paleness of her face worried him, making him want to conquer whatever terrified her. "What's going on, Caroline?"

Caroline swallowed visibly, doing her best to hide her obvious fear, but it was no use. Jax could smell the fear rolling off her in waves. "Could your sister shift?"

His eyes narrowed as he forced his eyes off her to stare over her head toward the radio, then back down at her. "Yes."

*******

"Alisha?" Caroline called out, looking away from the radio to stare around her. She walked through the Warriors to a corner and opened up a closet door to peer in, calling out to Jax's sister again.

"Is she okay?" Steve leaned over to whisper to Adam, but kept his eyes on Caroline, as did everyone else. "She's acting a little… whacko."

Caroline knew they all probably thought she was crazy, heard their whispered comments and felt their stares, but she didn't care. If she was right, this was really, really bad.

Lana glared at Steve as she passed, heading toward Caroline. "How can you be sure that was her?" Lana also looked around, searching. "Why would she come to you as a little boy and not herself?"

"A little boy?" Jax asked, understanding lighting his angry eyes. "The little boy who was here the night Blaze, Hunter, and I were here?"

Caroline gave a short nod, but kept her eyes from him. She knew she was going to have to bring up the dream. *Guess it's time to see which way Jax will go.* Unfortunately, she had a sick feeling that she knew exactly what his reaction would be.

"The dream I had. The little boy was there… in my dream." Caroline glanced around at everyone except for Jax. "And so was Mika."

"But that doesn't mean…," Lana began, but stopped and bit her lip when she made eye contact with Caroline.

"It's her," Caroline said without hesitation. "The little boy suddenly shows up as soon as Alisha disappears. Spirits can manipulate dreams. You know this, Lana. Someone is controlling her and my guess is Mika. The dream was a warning."

"You dreamt about my brother?" Jax asked, his voice compelling her to look at him. The rage boiling inside him was unmistakable as his eyes turned black as night.

"I didn't think it was a big deal," Caroline replied, but in all honesty, that was a lie. She'd known it was a big deal and had tried to keep it to herself. "With all the talk about him, I just figured that's what it was, but now I'm not so sure that's all there is to it. Could your brother control Alisha? I mean, would she allow that to happen?"

Jax didn't say anything for a few seconds as he stood, as if letting it all sink in; that, or he was trying to calm his rage. She wasn't sure which. "My brother is capable of anything and if he's threatened anyone, she would do anything to keep that person safe. She was, *is* a gentle soul."

Caroline figured as much, but needed to hear it. She bit her lip, knowing and dreading what was coming next.

"What was the dream about, Caroline, and do not lie to me?" Jax asked with clear warning.

Clearing her throat, she prayed she was wrong about Jax Wheeler. "I was being led down a hallway by a man in a white lab coat and into a large room, which now I realize was a morgue. There was a body on the table covered from head to toe. I kept asking the man who was under it, but he just gave me a smug, stupid grin and kept *tsking* in the back of his throat." She shivered as she remembered the dream that was still so clear in her mind. "I tried to get to the table but it felt like I was walking in sludge, but finally, I gripped the sheet. I was too terrified to pull it at first. The whole time, all the man did was stare at me making that awful *tsking* noise, before he turned silent as he watched me, as if in excited anticipation."

"Who was under the sheet?" Despite the softening of Jax's voice, it still held a dangerous edge.

"Before I could pull the sheet away, something touched my hand. It was the little boy. He was staring at me with so much sadness and shaking his head, as if telling me not to do it. Yet, I couldn't seem to stop myself. I had to know who was under the sheet." Caroline stopped again, her eyes going to Lana then Sid before looking quickly away.

"Who the fuck was under the sheet, Caroline?" Sid's voice made her cringe.

"It was you." Caroline looked back at Lana with such anguish she felt it to her very soul. She would never forget the picture of her sister on the cold steel of the table, bruised and beaten. "You had been..." She couldn't even bring herself to say it.

The growling coming from Sid was not easy to

ignore, but Lana did as she placed a comforting hand on Caroline's shoulder. "It was only a dream, Caroline. Nothing is going to happen to me."

"No, it was a warning." Caroline shook her head, wanting to finish this ugliness. "I looked up from you and the room was filled with tables that weren't there before. When a sinister laugh echoed in the room, a rush of wind blew the sheets away and you were all"—she looked around the room at the Warriors before her as she spoke—"on the tables, as well as your mates."

Caroline finally looked at Jax, who was staring at her, his eyes more black than anything she had ever seen, but his face remained emotionless. She wanted nothing more than for him to take her in his arms; just a touch of comfort from him.

"I pleaded for you to wake up," she told him, her voice wavering. "I begged. And then you did. You told me to run. When I didn't, you yelled, ordering me to run. I looked up toward the man who had led me to the room and right before my eyes he shifted to Mika. He started singing "Sweet Caroline" by Neil Diamond in such an ugly evil voice." She shuddered at the memory. "And I thought I hated that song before." She snorted, trying to lighten the very dark mood that surrounded her, but it didn't work. She knew her next words were going to send Jax away from her, and it tore at her heart more than she wanted to admit.

"What else?" Jax hadn't looked away from her; his

lips barely moved as he asked his two-word question. "Do not lie," he added as if reading it in her eyes that she thought about it.

She looked him straight in the eyes as she straightened her shoulders. "He raised a knife and began tapping his cheek, drawing blood. When a stream reached his mouth, he licked it and said..." She cleared her throat. "He had been wondering what I taste like."

"Is that all?" Jax's voice didn't sound human. It came from a deep dark place that neither Caroline nor anyone in the room had ever seen, she was sure of it.

"After that, everyone started yelling for me to run and I did. When I burst through a door into pitch-black, I woke up," Caroline added, hope filling her as Jax continued to stand and stare at her.

When Jax finally looked away, then turned to walk out the front door, her hopes were dashed... again. He was leaving. Anger so deep hit her with a force that propelled her out the door behind him.

"Where are you going?" Caroline actually jumped the steps trying to catch up with him. "Jax, wait."

When he continued to head toward his motorcycle without giving her any indication he was going to stop, her rage got the better of her.

"You're a coward!" she shouted, letting it all out. It didn't stop him, but it slowed him down. She could tell she'd hit a nerve when his shoulders tightened. He climbed on his motorcycle just as she stumbled up to him. "I didn't tell you about the dream because I knew you would do this. You would take off with some heroic notion that you're protecting me, us. But you're not. You're giving in to your brother and allowing him to run your life by keeping you away from people who care for you. Stop giving him that power, Jax."

Jax took his sunglasses off his handlebars and put them on before starting his bike.

She grabbed his arm, but he jerked it away as he used his boot to lift the kickstand. "If you do this, he wins… again. Please, don't leave." When the bike inched forward, Caroline stepped in front of it. "Please."

Jax looked away, his head shifting slightly, for a split second. When it looked like he was going to give in to her shameless pleading, he shook his head and, without a word, used his feet to back up his bike, turned, and took off without saying a word.

"Fuck you, Jax Wheeler!" Caroline screamed before picking up a rock and throwing it. She knew she was acting like one of her high school students, but dammit, she was pissed. She was beyond pissed; she was livid and hurt.

After standing staring after something that would never be hers, she turned to see Lana a few feet behind her. Her eyes shifted to see the Warriors back on the roof, doing their best to look busy, as if they hadn't witnessed the spectacle she had made of herself. All except for Sloan and Sid, who stood watching her closely from her front porch.

Lana walked up and put her arm around her, then pulled her into her arms for a hug she desperately needed. "It's going to be okay, Caroline." Lana whispered the soothing words as only a sister could do, but this time, they fell short. It wasn't going to be okay because her heart was already shattered.

## Chapter 7

Jax whipped in and out of traffic, his mind focused on one thing: Find Mika and destroy the bastard. He was done looking over his shoulder, waiting for him to make his move. He had let opportunities in the past go because he was his brother, but after Mika killed their sister that had all changed. He had disappeared until recently.

The traffic cleared and Jax opened up his bike to the max. Without having to watch stupid-ass drivers, his mind echoed Caroline's words to him as he left, but she had been wrong. He had been too enraged to say anything at that moment, his only thought to find Mika before he could harm her. Jax had no misconception that Mika wouldn't hurt her if given the chance.

Knowing exactly where he wanted to go, but not sure how to get there, Jax slowed and pulled over on the side of the highway. Taking out his phone, he found the directions to the club, Venue. Sloan would be pissed, but he'd have to get over it. No way in hell would he go through with the plan of letting Caroline be bait to draw Mika out, whether he was there with her or not.

Taking a second to memorize the directions, he put his phone back in his pocket. He didn't know if Mika would be there or not, but it was the only lead they had so he was going. Pulling back onto the highway, Jax wondered if the little boy really was his sister and why she would be shifting. Was Caroline right? Had his brother found a way to manipulate their dead sister? His rage built at the thought.

Pulling into Venue's parking lot, he was surprised by how full it was. It wasn't yet seven and the place was packed. He'd decided on the way there he would not shift. He was going to walk in, because if there was one thing his brother hated, it was a challenge, and that was exactly what he was there to do.

He parked next to other motorcycles and climbed off his bike. He kept his sunglasses in place so his eyes could roam freely. Even if the club were dark, it wouldn't matter. He would be able to see clearly. He felt the stares as he climbed the steps to the door of the club.

"It's a $10 cover charge," the large muscled man at the door told him.

Jax reached for his wallet, pulled out a ten, and handed it over without a word.

"Open the jacket," the man ordered after taking his money.

Jax opened his leather jacket so the man could see he had no weapon. He preferred carrying his gun in an ankle holster so he had no problem obliging the man, who looked bored as hell with his job.

"You're good." He motioned his head toward the

hallway that led into the club.

Jax walked down the dark corridor, his senses alert and ready for anything. His mind and body relaxed into that familiar zone of battle. He knew his eyes behind the sunglasses were black, his fangs felt thick in his mouth and yet, he kept calm. He was a born Warrior before he ever belonged to the VC Warriors. His life had started as a child learning to survive, to be the strongest in his tribe, and he had succeeded, just as he would succeed now in defeating his brother. No matter how long it took, he would defeat Mika, and in the process keep Caroline safe.

The music thumped through his body, everything hitting him at once as the corridor opened up into a huge room filled with people enjoying their night. His eyes behind the sunglasses scanned the faces, looking for only one. Someone bumped into him, but he didn't budge. It didn't faze him.

"Watch it, asshole." Some drunk turned to glare up at Jax.

Jax didn't even look at the guy, but growled, lifting one corner of his mouth long enough to show the guy his gleaming fang. It would be the only warning the fucker got. Obviously, he got the message, practically running over the girl who was with him. Jax turned his head, checking each side of him before he made his way to the bar. With no one to watch his back, he needed to make sure it was clear before he made himself vulnerable.

Even though he made his way slowly through the crowd, he moved with purpose. People sensed it, moving quickly out of his way as they whispered behind his back. This was good. Even if Mika wasn't there, he wanted to make damn sure his brother knew he had been. It wouldn't take long before word got around. It was time he stepped up his game. Caroline was already involved. There was nothing he could do about that except make sure she remained untouched by the bastard, and to get to Mika first.

It was time for his brother to die.

Reaching the bar, Jax ordered a beer, tuning his sharp hearing for his brother's voice. Odds, he knew, were not in his favor. If Mika was in the room, he'd already have his eyes on Jax, but Jax was ready and hoped Mika would fuck up and make a move.

"Hi." A beautiful brunette leaned against the bar and looked up at him. "I haven't seen you around here before."

Jax only glanced her way before turning his attention back to his beer and what was going on around him. Before coming to Cincinnati, he would have found the woman to be his type, but not anymore. Her makeup was so thick that she looked fake, not fresh and womanly like a certain teacher whose last words to him were, 'Fuck you, Jax Wheeler.' The memory actually made his lip curl in a half grin.

"You have a gorgeous smile. I'm really into vampires." She tried to sound sexy, but it was hard to do when you were trying to yell over the deafening music. When Jax didn't respond, she reached up to touch his hair. "And your hair is so long and black. Why don't you take off your sunglasses so I can see if your eyes are as sexy as that smile?"

Jax actually rolled his eyes behind his sunglasses, but before he could respond with a smart-ass remark to make her leave, a familiar voice spoke beside him.

"Tired of the little schoolteacher already, brother?"

\*\*\*\*\*\*

Caroline felt like a big piece of crap. She stood in her kitchen staring at her phone, wanting nothing more than to text Jax and apologize. She shouldn't have called him a coward in front of the other Warriors, it had just spewed from her mouth in a fit of anger. She'd felt guilty as hell since her anger had subsided.

"He'll be back." Sloan walked in, spotting her staring at her phone.

"I shouldn't have said that," Caroline admitted, looking from him back to her phone. "The coward part. I didn't mean it. Sometimes I have these moments where my mouth says stuff before my brain thinks it out."

"The 'fuck you, Jax Wheeler'?" Sloan eyed her with a grin.

"That I meant." Caroline nodded, then sighed and sat down, still holding her phone. "He's just so frustrating. Every time his brother is mentioned, he takes off thinking he's saving the world."

"Did you know that his brother killed their sister?" Sloan frowned, crossing his arms over his massive chest.

"What?" Caroline's head snapped up. A chill from deep inside trembled through her whole body, sending her standing up in shock. "Oh, my God. I knew she had been killed, but never knew it was Mika who killed her. Alisha never talked about it to me, but then I can't really blame her for that. How terrible." Tears filled her eyes as understanding swarmed her mind.

"Jax knows more about his brother than any of us, and his actions are justified." Sloan's frown softened. "I would be the same exact way. I don't know the whole story about his sister's death, but I can pretty much bet that he holds himself responsible. I understand the frustration, Caroline. I deal with a bunch of pain-in-the-ass Warriors, but if I were in Jax's shoes I would also do everything in my power to make sure you were safe, even if it meant leaving you. That's what Warriors are made to do. Keep the innocent safe."

Okay, she just went from feeling like crap to feeling

like the worst, most unappreciative person to ever walk the earth. Her tear-filled eyes looked up at Sloan. "I'm such a… bitch." As soon as the first sob escaped, it was impossible to keep the rest back. She dropped her head and sobbed, and they weren't nice little sobs, but ugly racking ones.

"No, you're not." Sloan reached out and tugged her to him. "Warriors are not the easiest to understand, except me. I'm different from the other assholes out there."

Things turned really ugly as she laughed, sobbed, and slobbered into his chest. Getting herself under control, she pulled away and looked up at the last Warrior she'd ever expected to comfort her. "You aren't…?" She stopped to find the right words.

"A bastard?" He chuckled before his face turned into the serious Sloan everyone saw all the time. "Oh, I am, Caroline. But I too have my moments."

"Sloan!" Adam ran into the room with Steve following.

"What?" Sloan's voice turned from caring to harsh in a second flat. He once again smiled down at her with a wink. "See… bastard."

Caroline watched in amazement as Sloan's whole façade changed in front of her very eyes. Before he turned toward Adam and Steve, the smile left his face, which was a shame. He was much more handsome when he smiled.

"Jax is going to Venue," Adam replied as Steve nodded.

"And how the hell do you know this?" Sloan headed toward them, an urgency to his tone.

"Because I read him." Adam looked a little sheepish when he answered, while Steve pointed at Adam, shaking his head.

"What's going on?" Sid walked in with everyone else following. "Adam and Steve took off like their asses were on fire."

"Oh, it's way better than that." Steve wiggled his eyebrows. "Tell them, Adam."

"Steve, go away." Adam nudged him.

"How in the hell could you have done that when he's not here?" Sloan demanded of Adam, but frowned at Steve, who was grinning like an idiot.

"Well, ah...," Adam started hesitantly.

"He can fucking read anybody, anytime... anywhere," Steve answered. "Ever since he's been turned he can do it. Holy shit, that feels good to let out. I suck at keeping secrets and that one was a fucking doozy."

"Is this true?" Sloan demanded. Caroline had no idea if he was happy with the fact or not.

"Yeah, pretty much," Adam replied with a shrug, looking really uncomfortable.

"What I want to know is when the fuck am I going to get some awesome powers? I mean, seriously, people. Jill can do the Carrie shit. Now Adam can lurk in our minds without us even knowing, which means I'll be thinking of naked men... a lot." When everyone looked at Steve oddly, he cleared his throat, rolling his eyes. "Not because I want to. Come on, I'm a ladies' man, but it will keep 'creeper boy' out of my head. Geez, can't say nothing around here without everyone taking it literally."

Sid took a few steps back with a frown, looking at Adam. "What am I thinking?"

"That Steve is a dumb ass," Adam's answer was spoken low.

Sid looked at Sloan with raised eyebrows. "I was blocking like a son of a bitch, boss. No way could he have read me, but he did without touching."

"That was your exact thought?" Sloan asked, sounding thoughtful.

"Steve is a dumb ass, yes." Sid nodded. "My exact thought."

"I think everyone gets the point." Steve huffed, rolling his eyes.

Caroline watched the Warriors and actually felt

sorry for Steve. Then a thought came to her. "Then you can read Mika." She took a step forward and knew they were all looking at her red swollen eyes, but didn't care.

"That's what I thought and I tried." Adam frowned, looking away from her. "I think it only works on people I've had contact with in the past. At least, I think that's the case. I've never had contact with Jax's brother."

"Why in the fuck haven't you told me about this?" Sloan demanded, his tone harsh.

Adam looked around before focusing on Sloan. "Because I don't want everyone thinking I'm prying into their shit, as Steve pointed out," Adam answered, then looked a little embarrassed. "The only reason I did with Jax is because I just wanted to let Caroline know he would be back."

Caroline's stomach dipped at hearing that and tears welled up again, but she held them back.

"And he plans on being back, but he's heading to the club right now to look for Mika," Adam announced.

"Let's go. If you can do this, really do this, you're getting a raise." Sloan headed toward the door.

"Well, ain't that a kick in the balls," Steve hissed with a sour look on his face. "You can invade our privacy, even Sloan's, and he gives you a fucking raise."

"If he even thinks about reading me without my knowledge, he dies." Sloan was right behind Steve so he heard every word, but then he stopped, looking at Blaze. "Blaze, stay here with Caroline."

"No problem." Blaze gave a short nod.

"No, I'll be fine." Caroline followed them out the door. "You might need him."

Sloan stopped and turned toward her. "Blaze is staying until Jax gets back."

"He's not coming back," Caroline replied, trying her best not to embarrass herself again.

Sloan shook his head, staring down at her. "He'll be back."

"And what makes you so sure about that?" Caroline bit her lip, wishing she hadn't asked, hating that it made her sound desperate. She looked away, but Sloan caught her chin, turning her face back to his.

"Because it's what I would do," he replied, before walking out the door.

Caroline stared at his retreating back in shock. Reaching up, she touched her face where his hand had been while watching as the group climbed on their bikes and hopped into cars. Blaze went back to the roof as she stood on the porch watching everyone leave, feeling more confused than ever.

## Chapter 8

Jax didn't even look Mika's way. He took a long swallow of his beer, finishing it off before gently placing the bottle on the bar. "What do you want, Mika?" Jax asked calmly, though inside he was primed and ready, wanting nothing more than to kill Mika on the spot. Too many innocent people were in the way, preventing him, so he couldn't make that move... yet.

"Oh, you know, the normal... mayhem, terror.... The list goes on and on," Mika said flippantly. "And what do you want, brother?"

Having no intention of playing Mika's game, Jax remained silent. His brother was conniving and very clever, but Jax knew him well, and that played in his favor.

"Hmmm, silence." Mika gave a nod and ordered a drink before turning on the stool toward Jax. "I bet I can answer my own question. Now, let's see, what does Jax want? I'd say number one on that list is vengeance, but then again, maybe not. It has been quite some time since the tragic death of our dear sister. Your priorities may have changed to, say, maybe a certain lovely creature who can talk to the dead and has a nice set of tits."

The only indication that Mika's words had any effect on him was the small tic in his jaw. Other than that, Jax remained outwardly calm, while on the inside, rage stormed through him, desperate for release on his brother.

"Ah, I see I've found that nerve." Mika chuckled before taking a sip of his drink. "Sweet Caroline. Yes, I know all about her and how she and her sister communicate with the dead. Pretty impressive. I would love to use her. I mean, talk to her about her special gift. I could put that to much use."

Just hearing her name spewed from the bastard's lips was enough to drive Jax insane, but he kept his composure. "Seems like you don't need her skill," Jax replied, keeping the fury out of his voice. "What did you threaten Alisha with?"

Mika's gasp was theatrical. "What are you insinuating…? Oh, okay, you caught me. I've already found my… what would you call it…? Dead people reader?" Mika actually looked thoughtful, then shook his head as a sinister grin spread across his face. "But you have to admit having our poor dead sister shift into a boy was genius. Hell, it took you all long enough. Did you know the dead could manipulate dreams?"

"Soon, you are going to die," Jax said without inflection, but this time, he looked straight into his brother's soulless eyes. "By my hands."

Mika wiped his mouth after draining his glass, then smashed it down on the bar. Shards of glass went everywhere, but Jax didn't move a muscle. "Is that a challenge?" Mika's voice turned from flippant asshole to hardcore evil. "I just love a challenge."

Jax was ready for the move and, as Mika went to sucker punch him in the side of the head, Jax shifted enough that the fist missed, sending Mika scrambling on the bar. With fluid ease, Jax grabbed Mika's hair, slamming his face on the hard surface before pulling him face-first down the length of the bar. People scattered out of the way, which was a good thing because Jax wasn't slowing down. He picked up Mika and pressed him against the wall. He gripped Mika around the throat and squeezed, lifting him up to where his feet didn't touch the ground.

"It's not a challenge, you sick bastard," Jax hissed, his face up close to Mika's. "It's a promise."

Mika futilely beat at Jax's arm. "I'm going to love...," Mika wheezed out, "fucking her while I squeeze... her throat."

Jax punched him in the mouth repeatedly. "You will never touch her," Jax roared, then threw Mika away from him.

Mika jumped up, wiping the blood from his mouth. "That's what you said about Alisha." Mika spat blood before looking up at Jax. Hatred painted his face. "But you failed her as you will fail the little teacher."

In three strides, Jax was in Mika's face as punches were thrown by both. It was a vicious fight, both men taking out their hatred for each other. Instead of releasing the pent-up rage, it seemed to grow with each hit smashing into the other. Grabbing Mika, Jax turned and body slammed him to the ground, but he lost his hold as Mika rolled, landing straddled on top of him, raining down punches. Jax took each hit, letting it fuel him.

With every ounce of strength Jax had, he flung Mika off him and jumped to his feet. Spitting blood, he wiped his mouth with a slow smile. "Is that all you've got?" Jax spat again. "You still hit like a bitch."

Mika roared, lunging for him, but Jax was quick with a spin kick to Mika's head, which sent him tumbling into tables. Jax followed, knocking tables out of the way, and noticed for the first time that the Warriors surrounded them.

"He's mine!" he warned as he reached for Mika, pulling him up and dodging a punch.

The momentum of the punch pulled Mika out of his grasp, but Sid was there to push him back in. The shift happened immediately. When Mika touched Sid, he shifted. Then he touched Jared and shifted again, trying to confuse Jax. Unperturbed, Jax's eyes tracked him until Jared repeatedly punched Mika in the face and yet, it was as if Jared was punching himself.

"Stop!" Jax yelled, but it was too late. Mika pulled Jared, knocking him into Sid as all three of them went down into a fighting pile. "Fuck!"

Jax headed over, trying to keep an eye on Mika who kept shifting from Sid to Jared. Damon and Sloan separated them. When they stood, there were two Sid's and one Jared, but no Mika.

"This shit is fucked-up," one Sid growled, staring at the other. "That is not me." He pointed directly at the other Sid.

"Fuck you, asshole." The other Sid growled back, trying to throw a punch, but Sloan stopped him. "No way could you pull off being me. Jax knows exactly who is who."

The fact was, Jax wasn't sure. Mika was good, damn good, but there was one way to find out. With a fluid motion, he reached behind him and pulled out the knife he always carried in the waistband of his pants, and with precise aim, threw it.

"Motherfucker!" one Sid bellowed, staring at the knife handle sticking out of his shoulder. "What in the fuck is wrong with you?"

Jax's eyes went straight to the other Sid, who stared at him wide-eyed before breaking away, running toward the door. Before Jax could reach him, Mika was outside, already shifted back to himself. He had grabbed a woman from the crowd and was holding her in front of him.

"If you come one step closer, I will break her

fucking neck." When Jax remained silent, Mika torqued the woman's neck, making her cry out. "You know I'll do it, brother."

"Then you will die." Jax's tone was matter-of-fact, knowing once again his brother had the upper hand. It pissed him the hell off.

"Please," the woman cried, her eyes begging Jax for help.

Jax sneered with a curse, unable to do a damn thing without endangering the woman. Neither his oath nor strength of character would allow him to do it.

"Watch your back," Jax hissed at his brother. "I'm coming after you." He pointed directly at him in warning.

"Big words, brother," Mika sneered.

"Why don't you let the woman go and face me like a man?" Jax knew Mika wouldn't let go of his shield, too afraid to lose, and lose he would, but it was worth a try; plus the more he got in the bastard's head, the better.

"Because I want you to suffer." Mika's face contorted with hatred as he backed his way through the crowd still holding the woman. "And I know you aren't afraid to die, but you do fear something happening to someone you care about. Alisha proved that." Mika finally pushed the woman free, then turned, rushing into the crowd, shifting from one person to the next as he fled, until he finally blended in with everyone else.

Jax's eyes tried to track Mika as he raced through the crowd, but it was useless. "Dammit," Jax cursed as he turned to head back toward the club, but found all the Warriors had been behind him the whole time. "Who's with Caroline?"

"Go search the crowd and make sure the woman is okay," Sloan ordered before answering Jax. "Blaze stayed behind."

"You son of a bitch." Sid stormed up to Jax, the knife still sticking out of his shoulder.

"You hit the wrong guy, dude." Steve was still standing there, his eyes going from Sid to Jax.

"I gave you an order." Sloan's growl sent Steve scurrying into the crowd.

"Do you think the chance of maybe hitting the wrong person, as you did in this case, was too big of a risk to take?" Sloan asked, his focus moving from the knife in Sid's shoulder to Jax.

"I'd say, fuck yes, it's too much of a risk to take," Sid growled. "It hurts like a bitch."

Slade had stayed behind also. He leaned close in concentration. "It's buried all the way to the handle." His eyes rose to Sid. "You want me to pull it out?"

"No, I'm going to wear it as a new piercing." Sid just gave him an "'are you serious'" look. "Fuck yes, I want it out."

"I need something to stop the blood." Slade looked around.

Jax figured since it was his fault, he should play nice. Taking off his jacket, he pulled off his shirt, tossing it to Slade. "Here."

Slade put one hand on Sid's shoulder, then gripped the knife handle with the other one. "I'm going to count to three."

"He's lying." Jill walked up at that exact moment. "It's two."

"Just pull the damn thing ou— FUCK YOU! That hurt." Sid grabbed the shirt out of Slade's hand and applied pressure. He walked up to Jax, getting in his face. "If you ever fucking throw a knife at me again, you are a dead man."

Jax casually pulled on his leather jacket. Not one to usually give explanations for his actions, he felt Sid deserved one. "Most shifters will lose their shift under the shock of extreme pain. I had a split second to decide."

"Well, you decided wrong," Sid grumbled, moving the shirt to look at his wound, which was already healing.

"No, I didn't," Jax replied, his voice gruff. "There was no wrong move. You just got screwed in the pick."

"Yeah, well fuck you and fuck your brother." Sid walked away, still pissed.

"Everyone needs to make sure to watch their backs." Jax ignored Sid's remark.

"Oh, is that what you were doing when you took off without a fucking plan?" Sloan's tone turned harsh. "We had a plan, which is now shot to hell."

"Caroline was not going to be part of that plan," Jax replied, not caring how pissed Sloan got. Caroline was not a Warrior and would not be a part of this any more than she already was, and he would make damn sure of that. "And Caroline is right. Mika has someone with the same gift as Lana and Caroline. He is manipulating Alisha to do his dirty work."

Sloan and Jax stood alone on the steps of the Venue. The crowd was dispersing as the human police had shown up. Damon and Duncan were filling them in on what had happened.

"What exactly does your brother want?" Sloan asked, his eyes searching.

"For me to suffer by taking out as many people close to me as possible, as well as Warriors he despises," Jax replied without hesitation. "And he won't stop until he succeeds or dies."

"Then he dies," Sloan responded with a single nod of his head. "You need to head back to Caroline's before I do."

"What the fuck is that supposed to mean?" Jax's head snapped up, his eyes narrowing in on his leader.

"Exactly what it sounds like." Sloan didn't back down. "Walk away from her and I will step in."

Jax took two steps, coming nose to nose with Sloan. "I'm keeping her safe, and fuck you for taking advantage of that."

"Any man would be a fool not to take advantage of that with a woman like Caroline." Sloan's words were like a slap to his face. "I comforted her after you left today, as a friend to you. If I comfort her again because you're being a total bastard with no clue, it will be as a man who has no respect for you."

Adrenaline rushed through his body, wanting more than anything to plaster Sloan Murphy on his ass, but he held back, still having some respect for his superior. "Touch her and I *will* kill you." He was still face-to-face with Sloan, each the same height.

"Hurt her, and *I* will kill you." Sloan cocked his eyebrow, challenging Jax's own words.

"Then you might as well kill me now," Jax spat in disgust. "Because the closer I get to her, the more in danger she is. She'll get hurt, even worse, killed."

"You are so full of shit." Sloan grabbed Jax's shoulder when he tried to pass, but Jax shrugged him off. Sloan was far from finished so he grabbed Jax again, pushing him up against the building. "What are you really running from, Jax? I never figured you for a pussy. If Mika is coming after her, he will come no matter if you're with her or not. He obviously knows your feelings. Who better to protect her than you?"

Jax pushed away from Sloan and walked away. He knew the son of a bitch was right and it pissed him off. Heading toward his bike, he ignored everyone in his path, yet kept his eyes open for his brother, who he knew was long gone. His fists tightened at his sides as Sloan's words echoed through his mind. What exactly was he running from when it came to Caroline?

## Chapter 9

Caroline headed up the unsteady ladder to the roof. Reaching the top, she looked up, spotting a hand hovering before her face. Taking it, she let Blaze help her the rest of the way up.

"Be careful and only walk on the new wood," he ordered, while searching for danger as she made her way to the peak of the roof and sat down.

Looking over her property, Caroline smiled, then closed her eyes, taking a deep breath. "I love it here." She peeked at Blaze then laughed. "I think I've said that a thousand times. Everyone is probably sick of hearing me say it."

"There's nothing wrong with being proud." Blaze nodded, sitting down.

Caroline shrugged then put her chin on her knees, staring out at the sunset. Loneliness swept over her, despite Blaze's closeness. It wasn't Blaze she wanted sitting next to her. "Yeah, you're right, and I am proud, even though there's still a lot of work to be done."

"It will get done," Blaze reassured her. "I should get back to working on this roof."

"You've done enough." Caroline lifted her chin to look at Blaze. "Why don't you let me make you something to eat? There's some leftover lunch meat.

I can make you a sandwich."

"No, I'm good." Blaze frowned and then looked over his shoulder to the ground below. "Why do you keep looking that way?"

Caroline shifted, her eyes rising to meet his, wondering if she should tell him. "I was just... ah...."

"How many are there?" His frown turned into a scowl.

"I'm sorry, Blaze." Caroline shook her head. "Sometimes it distracts me. We don't have to talk about it."

"How many?" he demanded.

"Six." She looked away from him briefly to the five dead men and one woman, who stood staring up at them. "Who are they?"

"You tell me?" Blaze shifted uncomfortably, looking over his shoulder, then back at her. "I see no one."

"I wish I could, but they haven't made contact with me. Actually, they don't seem to realize I can see them, or they just don't care." Caroline was dying to know who the people were. Five of them were badly burned, but the female had no burn scars that she could see. "And I won't make contact with them without your permission. I respect your privacy."

Blaze seemed to want to say more, but didn't, which made Caroline want to curse. She wasn't nosey by nature, but when she had dead people hanging around, it was primed in her to want to know who they were and what they wanted. And honestly, she was intrigued by Blaze and his unusual talent.

"Can you tell them to go the hell away?" Blaze grabbed a hammer, flipping it in his hand.

"I can tell them anything you want me to tell them, but that doesn't mean they'll listen." Caroline shrugged. "The dead do what they want."

"Doesn't that creep you out?" Blaze eyed her as he expertly caught the hammer he was tossing, but stopped, waiting for her answer.

"What? The dead?" Caroline laughed. "No, not really. There's evil in this world that creeps me out much more than they do. I'm used to it. Been seeing them since I was a little girl."

"That had to have been hard." Blaze once again glanced over his shoulder.

"It was until I found out that my sister could do the same thing." Caroline added, "We hid it from everyone, and each other, because we were afraid to say anything."

"Can they harm you?" Blaze again frowned at the thought.

Caroline shivered, thinking of not too long ago when she was pretty much held hostage after trying to read someone. "Physically, no, or at least not that I know of. They never have to this point." She stood carefully. "Mentally, yes, they can."

Blaze also stood, making sure she made it to the ladder safely. Helping her turn and holding her steady as she positioned herself on the ladder, Blaze was ready just in case she fell. "You need to not go up and down this ladder without someone here."

"Yes, sir." Caroline grinned up at him. "Now, I'm going to make you something to eat, so clean up or whatever, because it's getting dark and you've done enough."

"Yes, ma'am," Blaze mocked and actually gave her a full-on smile. She about fell off the damn ladder. Blaze was a handsome man, hands down, but when he smiled, he was breathtaking.

Knowing she was staring like an idiot, Caroline started down the ladder with a sad smile. Why did these Warriors all have to be so damn good-looking? It was so unfair.

"He'll be back," Blaze said from the roof, staring down at her.

Caroline stumbled at his words, but didn't say anything. Instead, she gave him a hesitant shrug as she made her way into the house, hoping with everything Blaze was right.

******

Singing quietly with the radio, Caroline got the lunch meat out, along with bread, mayo, mustard, and chips. She didn't know what Blaze liked so she just set it all out on the table. Grabbing a beer, she opened it and took a long drink. She was a wine drinker, but didn't have any so a beer would have to do.

Walking out onto the porch, she stood at the edge of the steps. It was now completely dark and she didn't hear Blaze moving around on the roof.

"Blaze?" she called out, looking up toward the roof. "Sandwich stuff is out."

"I sent him home." Jax's voice came from the darkness behind her.

Caroline jumped, almost losing her beer in the process. She squinted, trying to see him, but eerily, he blended into the darkness of her porch. "Why didn't you come in?" Caroline took a step closer, but stopped. "Why are you out here in the dark?"

He walked close enough she could finally see him.

"What happened, Jax?" She stared up at his bruised face—which looked like old bruising since he was already starting to heal—and swollen eye. Dried blood matted his hair. Her eyes moved down his body. He wore his leather jacket without a shirt. "Where's your shirt?" Not that she cared, because without a shirt while wearing that leather jacket, he was sexy as hell. She could stand there all night counting the muscles in his stomach.

"I gave it to Sid to stop the bleeding," Jax replied without further explanation.

"Stop whose blood?" Caroline gasped.

"Sid's," Jax replied evenly. "Slade needed it to stop the bleeding from the knife."

"Sid was stabbed? Oh, my God!" Caroline set her beer on the railing. "Is he okay? What happened? Who stabbed him?"

"He's fine," Jax replied, a frown forming across his lips. "And I stabbed him. Actually, I threw the knife that pierced him in the shoulder to the handle."

That took her aback for a second. Yet as she thought about it, Jax had to have a perfectly good reason for doing something like that. He didn't usually go on rampages stabbing his fellow Warriors, did he? *No, of course not*, she answered herself. "What did Sid do?"

Jax just stared at her, his eyes opened wide. "What did Sid do?" Jax laughed, but without humor. "I just told you I stabbed a fellow Warrior and all you can ask is 'what did Sid do?'"

"I think I know you well enough to know you wouldn't stab someone without good reason and Sid can,"—Caroline flipped her hand up in the air— "you know, piss people off. He just goes on and on and on...."

"Unbelievable." Jax shook his head, then rubbed his hand down his face.

Caroline's body started to heat. Her face burned and tingled, indicating she was getting pissed. She was even ready to apologize for calling him a coward, but as far as she was concerned, the way he was acting, he could forget an apology. The jerk.

"You know, if you just came to pick a fight, then you can just turn your ass around and leave." Caroline slammed her hand on her cocked hip.

"I'm bad news, Caroline." Jax's voice rose with each word. "Dammit! What in the hell will it take to prove that to you?"

For a split second, Caroline could have sworn she saw vulnerability he was trying so hard to hide. "No, Jax." Caroline shook her head. "Your brother is bad news, not you. What will it take for me to *prove* that to you?" She went to touch him, but he stepped away. The action made her heart ache and her jaw clench.

"You can't prove anything to me," Jax answered, not looking at her. "I know exactly who and what I am. You deserve better than what I can give you."

"Will you just please shut the hell up?" Caroline put

her hands on her ears and stomped her foot in what she knew looked like a tantrum. She took her hands from her ears and smacked him on his bare chest. "Damn you and your brother. Damn you and your… your tattoos. Damn you and your stupid guitar that you never taught me how to play, and damn you for making me care."

Jax just stared down at her with a look of stupid shock on his face as he absorbed each hard smack she delivered to his bare chest every time she said, "'damn you."'

Tears blurred her vision as she looked up at him. Removing her hand, she held it to her chest. "And damn you for coming back." She choked on a sob before turning around, slamming the door behind her, and then locking it.

# Chapter 10

Jax stood on the porch staring at the door that separated them. At that very moment, he knew without a doubt he could never let Caroline Fitzpatrick go. He was a selfish fuck because of it, but he couldn't walk away. Hell, how many damn times had he tried and always found himself back, just to be near her? Searching her out, hoping for a glimpse of her? Every single fucking moment of his fucked-up days she was in the back of his mind.

Grabbing her beer off the railing, he downed the rest. She was right. He was a coward, but not because he was afraid of his brother. That son of a bitch was going to die, and soon. No, he was a coward because he had never had feelings like this for anyone in his long life and it scared the hell out of him.

He was set in his ways. He could be a bastard and he knew for a fact he was not easy to live with. He had enemies, few friends, and didn't know how to express his feelings. She deserved someone else, and yet, even the thought of another with her threatened to send him in a killing rage. The only reason he hadn't killed Sloan earlier was because he knew Sloan, that tricky bastard, was just trying to get under his skin to make him realize exactly what he would be losing.

Looking through the window, he watched as Caroline stood in the middle of the room, not moving. She was beautiful and hurt, well, maybe a little pissed, which he couldn't blame her for. He pissed a lot of people off on a daily basis and usually he didn't care, but with her, he did care. Her tears did something to him that nothing had in a long time: they made him feel. *She* made him feel and he was becoming addicted to it, to her.

Setting the beer bottle back down, he tried the doorknob. It was locked. "Caroline, let me in." He could see her through the window of the door. "Caroline," he said a little louder, but she remained completely still, her back to him.

Glancing at the window, he knew he could open it and crawl through, but he shot that idea down. Instead, he used his shoulder and nudged the door hard, but it didn't budge. Okay, well that was a good thing because honestly, he'd thought a strong breeze would blow the damn thing down, but it seemed sturdier than he had first thought.

"Caroline, open the door," he called out, giving her one last chance to open the door for him.

"Just go away, Jax." He heard the tears in her voice. He watched as she angrily swiped them away from her face.

"Shit," he cursed, then leaned further back and used more of his strength to hit the door, which burst open and dropped off its hinges.

"You broke my door!" Caroline spun with a frown,

staring at her broken front door.

"I'll fix it." He walked up to her. "I wasn't done talking to you."

"Well, I was done talking to you." Caroline huffed, her face angry. "What else could you possibly have to say, Jax? Or do you just have to go over the list again of why you can't be around me? Who are you trying to convince, me or yourself? Because honestly, I get it. You don't want me, so using your brother is the best way to go about it."

When he attempted to speak, she held her hand up with a "'don't want to hear it'" attitude. "Save it." Caroline stopped him with a proud tilt of her head. "You need to fix my door and then leave."

Jax grabbed her hand, pulling her to him. Then, using his size and body to his advantage, he walked her backwards, plastering her to the wall and effectively boxing her in so she couldn't move. "I will fix your fucking door and I will leave when I'm damn good and ready, but first, you *will* hear me out."

"Why don't you just write it down, or better yet, I'll write it down since I know by heart what you're going to say," she hissed up at him, her face a beautiful shade of angry red.

"Oh, you think you know what I'm about to say?" Jax growled down at her.

"Yeah, I do." She narrowed her eyes at him, then lowered her voice, mocking his. "I'm no good for you. I need to stay away from you. You need to stay away from me. Blah, blah, blah."

A crooked smile tipped the corner of his mouth. "I don't sound like that and you have never heard me say blah, blah, blah."

She looked away from him, a tear escaping, sliding slowly down her cheek. "Let me go, Jax." Her voice sounded defeated.

"If only I could." Jax's voice deepened as he swiped the tear away.

"I can't keep doing this." Caroline's lip trembled, along with her voice. "I can't keep putting myself out there for you. You either want me or you don't."

Something inside Jax burned. It was a feeling he had never had and at that moment, he knew this woman meant more to him than his own life.

"That has never been the issue, Caroline," Jax whispered against her forehead. "The first time I laid eyes on you I wanted you, and that hasn't changed."

"Then why do you keep doing everything in your power to stay away from me?" Caroline asked, her eyes searching for the truth in his.

Jax struggled to keep his eyes off her lips, but at that question, he lifted his gaze to hers and he honestly didn't know how to respond.

"Is it really about your brother?" she probed, trying to get the truth. When he didn't answer, only stared at her, she sighed and tried to duck under his arm, but he stopped her. "Until you talk to me, Jax, this isn't going to work. I don't understand any of this, but I feel that this isn't just about your brother."

"I'm not one to talk about my feelings to anyone," Jax replied, knowing he sounded as uncomfortable as he felt. "Isn't it enough to know that I want you?"

Sadness flashed across her face before she bowed her head, hiding her features. "I wish it were, but I really don't know if it is."

This time, Jax let her go. Still standing with his arm against the wall, he stared blankly at where she had been, cursing himself. She was right. He was a coward.

\*\*\*\*\*\*

Caroline put the food away as Jax fixed her front door. It was so quiet she wanted to scream at the top of her lungs. She wished he would just leave so she could do just that. For a split second, she'd thought he was going to open up to her, but just as quickly, he shut down and closed up.

When he asked her 'if knowing he wanted her was enough,' she wanted to scream 'yes, it was enough,' and yet, she had held her ground. The truth was it wasn't enough. Not for her. Maybe for another woman it would be, but not her. She'd sworn after Rod that if she ever fell in love, it would be with the right man. Her eyes shifted toward Jax, knowing that he was the right man. Deep longing hit her, almost doubling her over. She loved him, that she knew, but the ass couldn't see it or did see it, yet just didn't love her back.

At least she gave him props for not lying just to get her into bed, because that was definitely where they would have ended up if he had lied. As she cleaned up, she watched him, the way his body moved, and wondered if she was a total idiot for not giving in. He took his jacket off, tossing it on the floor, and she had to bite her lip to stop the moan from escaping. He was a damn fine man. His shoulders were wide, his skin smooth and dark, not to mention the tribal tattoo that painted his back. Her fingers itched to trace each line.

Rolling her eyes at herself, she slammed the refrigerator door a little harder than necessary. Jax glanced over at her, but she averted her eyes from him. He had to go or she was going to cave. *Would that be such a bad thing?*

"Yes, you idiot, it would," she hissed to herself.

"What?" Jax turned from the door to stare at her.

She cleared her throat and then shook her head. "Nothing." Her eyes got a load of his shirtless chest, and all she wanted to do was cry. Every single hormone she possessed in her body pinged to attention, making her cringe.

"Don't you have a shirt or something?" Popped out of her mouth, and the slow grin spreading across his lips pissed her off. The ass knew he affected her. Hell, who was she kidding? Hadn't she told him more than once in the past hour she wanted him?

"No," he replied, his grin gleaming at her. "Why?"

Oh, no way was she answering that question. Heading to what was to be her bedroom, she rifled through boxes trying to find a shirt for the ass to wear. New rule: no shirt, no entry. Hey, it was her house and she could have that rule if she wanted.

Finding a shirt that had actually been Rod's, she grabbed it. It would be a little small, but it would be better than nothing, plus he didn't need to know it was Rod's. She was surprised she had anything left of Rod's, but it must have been mixed in with her stuff.

Heading back downstairs, she walked up to Jax holding out the shirt. "Here."

"What's that?" Jax looked at the shirt in her hand, but didn't take it.

"A shirt." She kept her eyes above his neck. She was way too close to him and her itchy fingers were getting trigger happy, wanting nothing more than to touch his bare skin.

His eyes narrowed dangerously. "Whose shirt is that, Caroline?" He still didn't take the shirt as he asked her that loaded question.

"It's... just a shirt." She'd hesitated, dammit. "You need a shirt, so here's a shirt."

Jax grabbed the shirt, still looking into her eyes. Ripping it in half with his bare hands, which was pretty impressive, he wadded it up and threw it out the door. The whole time, a muscle ticked in his cheek. Yeah, he was pissed.

"Didn't like the color?" she asked, trying to defuse the situation by being a smart-ass. Okay, so maybe handing him one of Rod's shirts to wear wasn't her brightest idea, but dammit, she was limited and he definitely wouldn't fit into one of her T-shirts. A half-naked Jax in her home was going to lead to her saying screw it and then screwing him, literally. It wasn't fair, dammit.

"Didn't like the motherfucker who wore the shirt," he replied, taking a step toward her.

"It's just a shirt, Jax." Caroline frowned, realizing that was probably a mistake and mean, if she wanted to be honest with herself.

"You have other shit of his here?" Jax demanded, his tone harsh.

"No." Was that jealousy she heard? "It must have been mixed in with my stuff when I packed to move."

"Don't play games with me." Jax loomed over her, the warning clear in his tone.

Caroline's head snapped back. "Well, that's calling the kettle black, now, isn't it?"

"What does that even mean?" Jax still loomed, his head tilted as he glared down at her.

"It means, you're the one playing games… not me." She huffed back at him.

"I'm not handing you other women's clothes to put on, now, am I?" Jax cocked one eyebrow at her, not giving an inch.

Okay, he got her there. *Think, Caroline, think.* "Well, no, but what do you care whose shirts I have hanging in my closet?" There, that should shut him up. "All you seem to do is want to get away from me. Oh, no… wait… you're back. Oops, no, there he goes again. Maybe he'll be back… maybe he won't. Tell me that's not a game."

"I told you I wanted you, dammit!" Jax shouted, then cursed again, obviously trying to keep his cool.

"So that should be good enough for me?" Caroline replied, wondering for a second if she wasn't being too hard on him, but why did she have to settle? Seriously, Jax settling between her legs would be heaven, but she wanted more from him. Not a 'wham-bam-thank-you-ma'am' moment before he took off again. Her heart and mind couldn't take it. She had settled once before just to have someone in her life, but not anymore. If he couldn't commit, he didn't get the goods. Screw that. "Well, it's not."

Jax opened his mouth to say something, but instead, a frustrated roar echoed throughout the room before he turned away, walking toward the door.

"Yeah, there he goes. Jax Wheeler, doing what he does best.... Exit left!" Caroline angrily yelled at his back, but then gasped when he slammed the newly fixed door with him on the inside.

Jax froze with his back to her, his shoulders tight. His whole body rigid. Then he turned around.

"I thought you were leaving... again." Caroline bit her lip as heat swept her body. "I, ah, thought...."

In three strides, he was in front of her and hauling her to him, his mouth smashing down on hers, successfully shutting her up. Pulling away, his lips inches from hers, he growled out, "You think too fucking much."

"Hey, I—"

He shut her up again, this time deepening the kiss as he tugged her body up against him. Her body relaxed into his, as if they were one. Again, he released her mouth and pulled away.

"What are you doing, Jax?" Her voice was a husky whisper.

"Do you ever shut up?" he hissed against her lips.

"Do you ever answer a question?" she shot back with a frown.

"I'm getting ready to show you exactly what Jax Wheeler is best at." The promise in Jax's voice was unmistakable.

## Chapter 11

Okay, that did shut her up. Seriously, did she hear him right, and what exactly did that mean? The lower part of her body throbbed in a pleasant, painful tempo, clearly understanding his meaning better than her brain did. *Stay strong,* she told herself, trying to be her own cheerleader. *Don't give in.* But feeling his hard body against her softness, the other part of her, the "'naughty need to get laid by this man'" part of her, was clapping happily, shouting, "'do it… do it… do it!'" My God, this man was going to make her a sex-crazed psycho.

His hand on her waist slowly moved up her side, resting just under her breast. She surprised herself when the word, "No," slipped past her lips.

*What?* Her mind screamed, but her mouth remained closed as she stood strong.

"No?" Jax actually grinned.

"I'm not a whore." That wiped the grin off his face, but she didn't care. "I've only been with one man, Jax. And that's because I knew he had feelings for me."

Jax took a step back from her, his eyes narrowing dangerously. "Have I given you the impression I thought you were a whore?"

Caroline sighed in frustration. "No, but with Rod—"

"Let's get something straight, right now," Jax interrupted her. "If you mention that bastard one more time, I will hunt him down and kill him."

"I'm just trying to explain." Caroline was somewhat shocked by his anger, yet her insides twisted excitedly at his alpha response to her mentioning her ex.

"You do not need to explain anything to me that involves that piece of shit," Jax sneered angrily. "I'm nothing like him. I would never raise my hand to you."

"I know that, but…." She was screwing up this whole conversation and didn't know how to express her feelings to the point he would understand her. She had never dealt with anyone like this man, this Warrior. It stumped her, as well as excited her in a weird way.

They both stood silent, staring at each other as if trying to figure out how to talk to one another.

Jax finally moved, running his hand down his face. "I've never been in a relationship before," he blurted, dropping his hand from his face. "I'm a loner, have always been a loner. I don't know how to take care of anyone other than myself. The more I tell you to stay away from me, the more I find myself here, by your side. I don't understand it. I can't fight it and I'm tired of fighting it. I used my psychopath of a brother as an excuse to stay away from you, not that the danger isn't real, but I can keep you safe and I know that, but that seems easier to blame than my inability to commit to any type of a relationship."

The words, "'oh, wow!'" jumbled through her brain as she listened to Jax. He was finally opening up to her, yet those two words were the only things floating around in her brain.

"I don't know where this will lead, Caroline." Jax frowned, his eyes burning into hers. "I don't even know if I'm capable of having any sort of a relationship, but with you, I will try, because it's what I want. If that isn't enough for you, then I really don't know where that leaves us."

Her heart swelled, realizing she'd seen a side to Jax that no one else had before, so much so it hurt. Knowing how uncomfortable Jax was, she knew she had to do something to ease his tension.

"That was painful, wasn't it?" Caroline gave him a small smile.

"You have no idea," he responded with no expression on his face.

"Thank you." She took a step toward him, but didn't reach out. "I'm not wanting to force an 'I love you,' a marriage proposal, or anything other than 'I'm interested in you for more than sex.' That's all, and I don't think that's too much to ask."

The only response from Jax was a low mumble or grumble, some kind of noise she couldn't quite make out.

"It's just the way I'm made, Jax." Caroline took another step closer to him. "And yes, it is enough for me. But can you please answer me one question?"

This time his response was a hard nod, his eyes narrowing again.

"How is it that a man like you has never been in a relationship?" Caroline's eyes swept his body before making it back to his eyes.

His eyes darkened. "Because I've never met anyone I enjoyed being around longer than a half an hour who was female." His answer was honest and to the point. "I've had sex with thousands of women."

"Excuse—" Caroline choked. "Did you say… thousands?"

"Well, I didn't keep count, but…." Jax tried to hide a grin.

This time it was Caroline's eyes that narrowed at his grin. She decided to give him a little of what he was giving her. "And really… a half an hour?" She cocked an eyebrow at him. "Not real impressed with those stats, Wheeler."

Jax laughed the laugh of a confident man, not intimidated by her jab at his sexual prowess as other men might be, and wasn't that a turn-on. "Well, you're lucky that I can tolerate you more than a half an hour, aren't you?"

"Yeah, we'll see about that." Caroline purposely tuned her voice to the husky channel, and the heat in his eyes had her reaching for her shirt.

******

If it were any other woman standing in front of him asking him to spill his feelings, he would have walked out with a 'fuck you' and not thought twice about it. But this woman was different, and for being the badass he thought he was, it scared the hell out of him.

He was already semi hard just from kissing her, which seemed to be the state his cock was in anytime he was around her, but as she reached for her shirt, pulling it over her head, his jeans became damn uncomfortable. He couldn't keep his eyes on hers. They had a will of their own as they roamed over her full breasts to her stomach, that wasn't completely flat, but slightly rounded as a woman's body should be.

When she tugged her shirt, which was still in her hand, back up to cover her bra, his eyes snapped back to hers. "Take it off," he demanded, knowing it would be the best time to let her know what kind of lover he was going to be. When she hesitated, he frowned. "Now, or you'll be buying a new one."

Even though she reached around to do as he ordered, her mouth opened and the look on her face told him she had something to say about his demand and consequence.

"Do not argue with me." Jax growled the warning. "If you want me, then this is how it is."

"And I wouldn't want it any other way," Caroline shot back, surprising him. "But I was going to say, you would be the one buying me a new bra if you tore this one. They're not cheap."

Caroline continued to shock the hell out of him, but he kept his calm façade, which was about to fucking kill him. He wanted nothing more than to unleash his hunger for her, but used his control to be patient, so she could have the pleasure he knew he could deliver. If he ripped her clothes off, bent her over and fucked her like he wanted to do, then the pleasure would be all his. Another day, he would do just that, but not today. Not their first time.

He watched as she expertly unhooked her bra, sliding the straps down her arms until she was exposed to him. Her skin was smooth and pale, making her large dark nipples stand out. They puckered invitingly at his gaze.

"I know they're big." She cleared her throat self-consciously, but didn't cover her breasts as he expected. "I know most men like smaller women, but—"

"Shut up." His order wasn't spoken harshly. He used his thumb to touch one nipple before leaning down, taking it into his mouth for only a second, and then gave it a small pinch. "Most men are idiots and I'm not most men. From here on out, I'm the only man you need to please and, believe me, Caroline, when I say I'm more than pleased."

Jax took her hand, placing it on his cock through his jeans. He knew he was a big man, not that he compared himself to others, and when her eyes widened, he knew for a fact that any comparison between him and that bastard would be in his favor in this area and yeah, as a man, that made him harder than stone. His cock actually jerked, a miracle considering how snug he was in his jeans.

He removed his hand and was happy when she kept her palm on his hard bulge. Her tongue snaked out, wetting her lips, and she looked down, watching her own hand rubbing against him. Slowly, her hand made its way to his stomach, to his chest and back down, feeling her way back to his throbbing cock. Without asking, she knelt and unbuttoned his jeans, and he allowed it. In truth, he was afraid he was going to be seriously injured if his pants didn't get loosened. Once unbuttoned, she pulled his zipper down using extreme caution, which he was thankful for, but his eyes didn't leave her. The passion in her face was something he had never really seen on another woman's features, and it blew him away.

Almost all the women he could remember wanted him, and yet it was different. They would strip for him, but the way Caroline did it felt pure with no hidden agenda other than pleasing him. The women he had known were beautiful and knew it, but Caroline didn't see that in herself, though she was the most beautiful woman Jax had ever touched. During his musing, she had gently pulled out his cock, stroking before she stuck out her tongue, swiping the precum from his tip.

"Fuck, girl." He bent, lifting her. His jeans were up, yet the tip of his cock teased her stomach. "More of that later," he promised.

Caroline smiled eagerly before reaching out and running her fingers down his chest, over his tattoos. "They're beautiful."

"You damned them not fifteen minutes ago." His eyes and hands caressed her breasts, but a small smile tipped his lips.

"No, I love tattoos." Caroline moaned when he pinched her nipple, giving it a tug. "I was just angry because the first time I saw you at the compound without your shirt, I saw your tattoos and never stopped thinking about them, or you."

"Hmmm, really?" Jax worked his thumbs into the waist of her yoga pants, which fit her like a fucking dream, and as he worked them down, he kissed and licked across her skin, stopping for a long time to suck on her breast. The more she moaned, the harder he sucked. His hand worked around to the front of her panties, soaking wet from her need, which he could also smell. The smell of a woman's arousal had always turned him on, but Caroline had a special scent that drove him to the edge.

He hooked her underwear, pulling them down with her yoga pants until she stood in front of him totally naked. Her thighs were rounded and strong enough to squeeze. A man couldn't ask for more. His hands ran from her thighs to the ass he had stared at all day in those fucking yoga pants. Caroline's body was proportioned just right. Big tits and ass, with some beautiful flesh in between. She was womanly and beautiful. Jax knew he should tell her what he felt about her body, but he didn't know the right words for a woman like her, so his best bet was to show her. He was a harsh lover, a demanding lover, an honest lover, but one thing he knew for sure, she would never walk away from his bed disappointed.

He stood and picked her up, heading for the steps, but stopped. "Where's your bed?"

"In my bedroom, but it's not put up yet. I haven't had time yet." Her eyes were hooded as she looked up at him. "We don't need a bed."

Jax kissed her hard before looking around. "You need curtains," he mentioned as he spotted her mattress in the corner. He headed that way, laying her down, then checked to make sure they wouldn't be in view of prying eyes. Satisfied, he brought his attention back to her.

He couldn't stop looking at her, drinking her in. Her eyes told him everything he needed to know. She was ready for him.

"Your eyes are black," she whispered, her hands reaching up to caress his face.

"Does that bother you? That I'm different than a human man?" Jax let her hands roam, giving her time to adjust to the feel of his body, even though he was not inside her yet. His hands moved from her neck down her shoulder to caress her breasts as they slowly moved down the curve of her stomach to between her legs. With one thrust, he slipped a finger inside her, moving it gently before adding another.

"No, not at all." She moaned, her body rocking with the tempo he set as she tilted her neck in sweet offering. "You can have a taste if you feel the need. I've heard you guys like to do that when having—"

Jax growled at her words, cutting her off. He would love to sink his teeth into her soft flesh, but that would wait for another day. She was on the edge, as was he. Spreading her legs wider, he positioned himself, his cock poised at her sweet opening.

"Look at me, Caroline," Jax demanded. When she obeyed, he slowly pushed inside her, forcefully, but gently enough to allow her to accommodate his size. "Jesus, you're tight."

"Is that a compliment?" Caroline moaned the last word as he pushed, sheathing himself fully inside her warmth.

"Fuck, yes," he hissed, still staring down at her,

wanting to see every expression on her beautiful face as he took her. He made damn sure that every thrust was pleasurable for her, with touching, kissing, licking, or sucking. Whatever it took he did, because that was the kind of lover he was, except never in his past had he been in complete awe of the woman who lay under him. Even though he made sure the women of his past left his bed satisfied, he forgot them as soon as the door closed. This was going to be much different.

With each thrust, Caroline met him with fierce determination to give him as much pleasure as he was intent on giving her; he could read it on her face, in every touch and the way she responded to him. She wrapped her legs around his waist, helping him sink deeper inside her, and that was all it took. He reached between her legs, pinching and caressing, because no way in hell was he going to ride this wave alone. She would be riding it with him.

# Chapter 12

Sloan looked at the clock then to the door. "Has anyone heard from Jax?"

"Since he stabbed me, no." Sid's angry answer indicated he had not forgiven Jax.

"Give it a fucking rest." Jared snorted. "It's been two fucking days and you're a damn vampire. You were completely healed within half an hour."

"Fuck you, Jared," Sid hissed, then threw a knife at him.

Jared blocked the knife. "What in the hell are you doing?"

"Hey, it's no big deal. You're a vampire. It'll heal in half an hour," Sid shot back. "Asshole."

"Throw a knife at me again and I'll—"

"Why don't I just have Damon decapitate both of you so we don't have to hear your shit anymore?" Sloan glared at them both while Damon cracked his knuckles. "Because honestly, I'm sick of hearing it."

The door opened and Jax strolled in.

"Oh, well, what the fuck!" Sloan threw his hand up. "So nice of you to follow fucking orders and be here on time. Are you sure I'm not intruding on your day?" Sloan studied Jax and while he wasn't sure, he would pretty much bet he had been with Caroline. And if he really wanted to lay some money down, he'd bet that Jax seemed a little more relaxed, a sure sign the fucker had been laid. Sloan hid a smile, wondering if his parting remark to Jax about Caroline hadn't lit a fire under the Warrior's dumb ass. About fucking time. Sloan didn't hide his grin at that thought.

"Actually, it is pretty hectic so if we can hurry this along...." Jax leaned against the wall, crossing his arms across his chest and glaring at Sloan before glancing toward Sid. "How's the shoulder?"

"Fuck you." Sid sneered his way.

"His shoulder's fine, but his butt hurts." Jared grinned at his own joke. "Get it? He's butt hurt."

Steve laughed the loudest. Actually, he was the only one who laughed other than Jared.

"I will kill you." Sid turned to Steve.

"He said it." Steve pointed at Jared, not laughing any longer.

"Where have you been?" Sloan asked Jax, ignoring Steve.

"I covered my shift." He nodded at Blaze. "Other than that, I think that's all you need to know."

"Fair enough, because I really don't give a shit what you do on your time, but I just had a meeting with all the pack leaders in the area and your time is going to become my time." Sloan grabbed folders, handing them to Jill to pass out. "They need our help. Since their laws have become nonexistent for shifters since the shit storm Hunter caused, we're going to be doing double shift."

"We already do double shift." Adam groaned. "Why in the hell can't they train other shifters like we do with vampires?"

"They are, but that takes time. It seems the shifter from the other night was right. Shifters, your brother among them, are trying to form their own councils. Without regulation, this could mean a true battle between us and them." Sloan frowned, glancing at Jax. "And that brings me to my next point."

"Which is?" Jax took the folder from Jill, but his eyes were on Slade.

"You and Blaze are going to head up the training, which starts tomorrow. In the folders are the candidates with all their information," Sloan explained. "When the others are free, they can help you. I sent Dillon down to Kentucky to work with the pack leaders in that area. Hunter's going to show him around, introduce him. I may be sending more, but we will see what Dillon reports back to us. He's pretty good in the field and makes a lot of contacts."

"And who exactly are we training?" Jax's eyes

narrowed as if already knowing the answer.

"Vampires and shifters. Actually, anyone who will apply." Sloan didn't hesitate in his answer. "We're being overrun. We need to keep control of the situation. We're going to help them train shifters until they can get a grip on it, but they will be under VC rules and regulations. Anyone breaking our laws will be arrested, whether they're vampires, humans, or shifters."

"I have no problem with it, but Caroline cannot be left unguarded." Jax glanced around at all the men. "None of the women should be left unguarded."

"I agree and we'll figure it out." Sloan had already thought of this. "When does school start?"

"It usually starts in late August," Adam answered. "Which is only two weeks away."

"So if Mika isn't taken care of by then, we need a plan," Sloan replied, looking toward Jax. "Any ideas?"

The only answer Jax gave was a frown.

"Me, Adam, and Steve can act as students in her class," Jill offered, looking at both Steve and Adam, who nodded in agreement.

"I've heard they've integrated the humans and vampires in the same classrooms," Adam added. "I'm in."

"Going back to high school." Steve grinned widely. "Holy shit, finally an undercover job."

"You agree with that?" Sloan asked Jax.

"It's not like any of you could pass as high school students," Jill replied when Jax hesitated. "We know what we're doing, Jax, and it will be three of us. Being the girl of the three I can follow her into restrooms. With Adam and Steve plus me, if something does go down, then one of us can always be guarding her."

"Yes, while I'm kicking ass and taking names, Jill can guard the teach," Steve said with self-importance.

Jill snorted and rolled her eyes at him. "You wish."

"At this point, it seems the only plan we have." Jax nodded, not totally agreeing or disagreeing.

"I'll set it up." Sloan made a note on a piece of paper.

"You really need a secretary," Jill mused, watching him.

"No." Sloan didn't even look up from the paper.

"Why not?" Jill continued to press the issue. "Your desk is a mess, you're always answering the phone, and by the way, my pay was late in my account."

"Yeah, so was mine," Steve piped in. "That really needs to be taken care of. I got bills now. I think a secretary is a great idea."

"I think having someone organized would help you so you can focus on important things," Jill continued her case.

"There is no woman on Earth who wouldn't be running out of this office screaming and crying by the end of the first day." Sid snorted. "Shit, I'll put money down on that. Anyone care to make that bet?"

No one even reached for their wallets because they all knew that there probably wasn't a woman alive who could handle Sloan Murphy.

Sloan glared up at Sid, but then realized he was probably right. "If you're not happy with the way I run shit, get the fuck out."

Jill rolled her eyes at his blustering. "That's not what I mean."

"Ah, hey, man. You're doing a great job." Steve laughed nervously. "I was just… I mean hell, man… I'd do this job for no pay."

"That can be arranged," Sloan warned.

"Jill, shut up and leave Sloan alone." Steve glared at her. "He doesn't need a secretary. He does a great job."

"Hey, kiss ass, shut up," Jill replied, but kept her eyes on Sloan. "If I can find the perfect candidate, will you at least talk to them and give them a chance?"

Sloan sighed, leaning back in his chair. "You're not going to let this go, are you?"

"Probably not." Jill beamed a smile of victory at him. "You're going to be thanking me, Sloan."

"I seriously doubt that," Sloan grumbled before kicking them all out of his office. "I need a fucking vacation."

\*\*\*\*\*\*

Caroline sat in the large compound kitchen with Lana, Nicole, Pam, and Tessa, drinking coffee, but her mind was elsewhere. Last night had been nothing like she had ever experienced before, and waking up in Jax's arms had been pure bliss. Sipping her coffee, she looked up to see all the women staring at her.

"What?"

A huge smile spread across Lana's face. "You had sex."

"Definitely." Tessa grinned, then laughed.

"Well, spill it, woman." Nicole leaned toward her.

"I don't know what you're talking about." Caroline's face grew warm with embarrassment.

"You know exactly what we're talking about so don't try to fool us. We know the look of a woman satisfied by a Warrior and, woman, you're wearing that look all over your face." Pam laughed, giving her a knowing look. "Sitting there all dreamy-eyed with a *satisfied* smile. So how is Jax Wheeler in the sack?"

"You guys are terrible." Caroline stood up quickly to pour herself some more coffee, then turned back toward the women. "And a real lady never tells."

"No ladies at this table, and I know for a fact you aren't one either." Lana snorted, rolling her eyes. "So start talking, sister."

Thank God Jill picked that moment to barge in the door. "You guys are not going to believe this." Jill grabbed a chair, sitting down quickly and glancing at the door. "We are going to find Sloan a secretary."

"He agreed to that?" Nicole looked doubtful.

"In a Sloan kind of way." Jill's mischievous grin grew. "So you guys with me on this?"

"Hell yeah, we're in." Tessa nodded with determination. "It's about time we get Sloan organized."

"And laid," Pam added and then glanced at Caroline. "Seems Sloan is the only one not getting laid."

Jill's eyes followed Pam's gaze to Caroline, who was blushing furiously. "Finally." Jill laughed excitedly. "Took him long enough."

"I could eat the ass end out of a skunk I'm so hungry," Steve was saying as he came through the door.

"And Steve," the women said at once, then burst out laughing.

"Ah, shit, what did I walk into?" Steve actually looked scared as he stared at the women.

"Nothing at all, Steve." Nicole stood, patting Steve on the cheek. "Soon we'll be helping you."

"Helping me what?" Steve asked, as if he didn't know whether to laugh, cry, or run. When the women didn't answer, Steve looked around, frantic. "Help me what?"

Caroline laughed, but stopped when Jax walked in, his intense eyes searching her out and finding her. Every part of her body that could tingle did and with a force that had her biting her lip. The women became very quiet, watching. "You ready to go?"

Nodding, Caroline stood, taking her cup to the sink and washing it out.

"So, Jax." Lana used her cop voice. "Where were you last night?"

Pam, Tessa, Nicole, and Jill all stared at him with questioning eyes and knowing smiles.

"Lana, stop," Caroline warned, hurrying toward Jax, whose narrowed eyes were zoomed in on Lana. "Let's go." She tried to pull Jax, but he wasn't moving.

"Jax, man, I would run and run fast," Steve warned, eyeing the women. "They're acting crazy, and it seems their interest just went from me to you."

Jax walked over, bending down so his hands were on the table as he leaned toward Lana. "You want to play this game?" Jax tilted his head, looking straight at her. "Because honestly, if you want to play the cop, I'll tell you exactly where I was, who I was with, and what I was doing. But I think we both know we don't want to embarrass your sister any more than she is now. Do we, Officer Fitzpatrick?"

Caroline watched in awe as Lana obediently shook her head and shut up, she didn't even correct him that her name was now Sinclair and the fact she wasn't technically a cop anymore since she worked with the Warriors instead of the police force. Jax straightened, moving away from the table, his eyes pinning Lana to the spot before he took Caroline's hand in his, heading for the door.

"Holy crap, that was hot," was the last thing

Caroline heard Jill say as the door closed behind them. And Jill was right, it was hot and she hoped to hell Jax was taking her back to her place.

## Chapter 13

Jax did take her home and they hardly made it through the door before he was inside her. They had taken her car instead of his motorcycle to the compound because of the rain. Once in the car, she had been hesitant to do anything, but she had just happened to glance at his lap to see he was hard. That was all the encouragement she needed. The short drive gave her opportunity to drive him insane with her hands and mouth.

Pulling into her drive, he slammed on the brakes and tucked himself back into his pants. "You're damn lucky we made it back alive." Jax opened the door, got out, and helped her to her feet.

Caroline grinned up at him, noticing he wasn't looking at her, but scanning the area. Most women would probably be upset because his attention had been diverted, but she wasn't. He was a Warrior and she knew this was just who he was. He was making sure it was safe and as far as she was concerned that was sexy as hell, plus he was with her and not running away. Everything about the man was hot and she wanted him with a passion that made her knees weak.

He led her up to the porch, unlocked her door, and went in first, stopping to listen and scan. Satisfied, he pulled her inside and shut the door, locking it. His mouth smashed down on hers so fast it took her breath away. He pulled her up so she straddled his body, both hands gripping her ass, grinding her into him.

Lifting her up higher, he ordered her to take off her shirt and bra, which she did quickly. His strength to hold her at the height he could suck and lick each of her breasts amazed her because she wasn't a petite girl.

"This is going to be hard and fast." He growled the warning against her stomach before setting her down. He quickly had her naked before him and had freed his cock from his jeans without taking them off.

That morning before leaving, she had hung her curtains at his request while he'd brought some of her furniture in from the barn. Carrying her over to the kitchen, Jax sat her down and turned her. She placed both hands on the counter. He used his booted feet to carefully nudge her legs apart before leaning over her with his body. His hardness pressed against her ass, sending bolts of desire racing through her. He then used his fingers to make sure she was ready for him.

His breathing was rough against her ear and she loved the sound of it. It was the sound of Jax wanting her and she savored every second of it. She gasped and moaned in one breath when he pushed inside of her in one swift movement. Her arms straightened as she gripped the counter. His hands were everywhere, the overwhelming pleasure they gave her almost too much. Slamming into her, he picked up the tempo; an arm went around her stomach while his other hand rested beside hers on the counter to keep her from slamming against the hard surface.

His power surrounding her combined with his pounding into her was overwhelming. Darkness edged her vision, but she fought it. No way in hell was she missing out on this by passing out. He had said this was going to be hard and fast—hard was right, but fast wasn't the case. Jax's stamina shocked her, but in a good, delicious way.

Knowing she was on the edge, Caroline locked her legs and gripped the counter until her knuckles turned white. And then it hit. Wave after wave of release slammed into her and it took everything she had to stay on her feet.

Jax must have felt it also, but once he gently pulled out and re-snapped his pants, he picked her up, carrying her to the couch. Caroline watched his face carefully. Something wasn't right.

"What's wrong?" She tried to turn his face toward hers, but he remained staring straight ahead.

"I shouldn't have taken you like that." Jax's voice was low, filled with disgust.

Naked, Caroline shifted and crawled up on his lap so she straddled him. She put both hands on his face. "I don't know why not. I obviously thoroughly enjoyed every second of it." She smiled, but when he didn't return the gesture, she leaned back. "And I hope you do it again and soon."

"You deserve something more than me fucking you on your kitchen counter." Jax growled, finally looking at her.

"You have got to be kidding me?" Caroline's temper rose, simmering. "So what you're saying is it's okay to *fuck* me on my living floor four times—"

"Five," he broke in.

"Excuse me, five times, but it's totally uncalled for to *fuck* me in my kitchen," Caroline spat out. "Then I guess I can't suck your dick again while you're driving since I'm such a lady."

Something glimmered in Jax's eyes before it was gone. "No, that's perfectly fine," Jax gave the typical male response.

Caroline sat in shock until a smile tipped the corner of his lips. "You're an ass." She smacked him on the chest, fighting to get off his lap.

Jax flipped her over onto the couch, lying across her to keep her still. "You're different, Caroline."

"Good, because I don't want to be like the other *thousand* women you've been with, asshole." Caroline wiggled, trying to dislodge him, but it was no use. He wasn't budging.

"That's not what I meant." He frowned down at her. "I don't want you to think I don't..."

"Respect me?" Caroline finished when he hesitated.

"Yeah, I guess that's it," Jax replied, not looking too happy with the conversation.

"Jax, there are so many ways to disrespect me, but what we did in the kitchen definitely isn't one of them." Caroline was understanding Jax a little more. Even though he was closed off, he was opening up to her slowly, to where she was learning to read him. "I'm going to take a leap here and say that anything you do to me during sex will not make me think you are disrespecting me and, if I feel that way, I promise to tell you."

"Yeah" was his only response, but relief seemed to sweep across his handsome features.

"Thank you." She smiled up at him.

"For what?" he asked, confusion evident in his voice.

"For caring enough about something most men wouldn't even think about." She kissed his chin.

"And once again, I'm not most men." He growled down at her.

"You most certainly aren't," she agreed, tracing his

lips with her finger.

"Now say it again," he demanded with a growl, but a teasing gleam in his eye.

"Say what?"

"Suck my dick." He laughed when she smacked him. "I can't believe my little teacher says words like that. And the things you do would shock the teaching world."

"You'd be shocked at what this teacher would do for you." Caroline made sure her voice was husky when she replied.

"I doubt it, but I'm more than willing to let you try." Jax grinned down at her before taking her mouth in a kiss that set her soul on fire.

\*\*\*\*\*\*

While Jax put together her bed, Caroline started painting the living room. She couldn't wipe the smile off her face as she rolled paint on the wall, happily humming. A loud knock from the front door startled her and before she could turn around, Jax was coming down the steps opening her front door.

"What's up?" Jax said, stepping aside so Blaze and Sid could enter.

"Sloan put me on the training job with you guys

and..." Sid glanced over at Caroline, a large frown on his face.

"And what?" Jax also glanced at Caroline, who just shrugged.

"And Lana wanted me to come here and make nice." Sid sneered and then pointed at Caroline. "Hush!"

Caroline used the roller to point to herself in total innocence. "I didn't say a word."

Sid turned his attention back to Jax. "So I accept your apology for stabbing me."

"I don't think I apologized for that." Jax cocked his eyebrow.

"Well, fuck you, you should have." Sid growled before calming himself down and waited a second, as if recalling what he was supposed to say. "I understand why you did it."

Caroline watched in awe as Sid seemed to struggle with his words. She held the roller up to hide her grin.

"So apology accepted," Sid finished, looking relieved.

"Again, I don't think I apologized." Jax didn't budge on the fact so Caroline decided to step in.

"There's coffee and beer as well as leftover—" she started to say, but yeah, Sid wasn't finished.

"Dude, I'm on the edge here." Sid eyed Jax. "And if this don't get settled, I'm going to have one pissed-off woman on my hands. So take this however the fuck you want to take this. I don't care, taking one for the team. I have in the past, but if you ever throw a fucking knife at me again, Slade will not be able to…"

Caroline watched Jax's eyes darken then glanced at Blaze who was watching with a half grin, casually leaning up against the wall without a care in the world.

"He gets it." Caroline hurried between them. "Don't you, Jax?"

"Oh, yeah." His tone was even, but harsh. "I get it."

"Good, because if you ever and I mean ever—" Sid growled.

"Oh, for shit's sake." Caroline threatened them both with her roller full of paint. "Stop acting like two-year-olds before I put you both in time-out. Now shake hands."

When they both just stared at each other, Caroline swung her roller around.

"I said shake before I clobber you both with this roller." She watched as they grasped hands, but then they wouldn't let go. She looked down to see both of their hands gripped in a painful handshake war. Glaring at Blaze, who was still watching with an amused grin on his face, she said, "Will you please do something before I clobber you too? Don't think I won't."

Blaze pushed himself off the wall and then stepped between Jax and Sid. When he couldn't get them to part, he laid his hands on both their wrists until finally, they shot apart.

"Holy shit, Blaze." Sid grabbed his wrist. "That fucking hurts."

"Yeah, it does," Blaze agreed with a grin. "Now, can we talk about what we came here to talk about without you two going at each other or Caroline beating me to death with her paint roller?"

Caroline went back to painting, but kept a close eye on Sid and Jax. Finally, they seemed to calm down and were working on whatever it was Warriors worked on.

"While Sid and Blaze are here, I'm going to have them help me move some more furniture in from the barn and then we'll work on the roof. Is there anything special you want brought inside?" Jax had walked up behind her, startling her.

"You scared me." She laughed when she jumped. "If you can get my dresser and the two smaller nightstands that go beside the bed, that would be great."

"No problem." He winked at her, turned and walked out with Sid and Blaze following.

She went back to work with a smile, remembering only a few short weeks ago she had bought this house thinking she would be here alone. It was amazing how things worked out. With a frown, she looked toward the front door, thinking she heard footsteps. When no one knocked, she put the roller down and headed that way. She could have sworn she'd heard footsteps. Opening the door, she was shocked beyond speech.

"Why haven't you answered my calls, Caroline?" Rod stood on her front porch looking pissed and as intimidating as ever. "I've called and called and called. Thankfully, one of your schoolteacher friends told me where you moved to. Obviously, you've been busy. I really wish you had waited for me to make a decision as big as buying our home. But with a lot of work we can turn this dump into a nice place for our family."

"Why are you here, Rod?" Caroline was still in a state of shock, his words not fully registering. She tried to close the door a little, but he stopped it with his foot.

"Why, to take you back." Rod smiled at her. "To give you a second chance."

# Chapter 14

Finally, Rod's words registered and she saw red. "To take *me* back?" Instead of trying to slam the door shut, she forced it wide open. "To give *me* a second chance? Are you out of your mind?" She stomped toward him, pushing up her sleeves.

"Now, Caroline," Rod said, taking a step back. "I know we left things on a bad note, but I've given you time to see your mistake. We can make this work."

"My mistake? Make it work?" Caroline growled, unable to stop repeating his absurdity. Her eyes spotted movement behind Rod. "And you brought your brother with you? Why, so he can hold me down while you beat me?"

"Hi, Caroline." Fred waved to her from the front yard.

"You're out of your mind coming here." Caroline ignored Fred. "Get the hell off my property! You're lucky I didn't press charges of abuse the first time. Don't think I won't do it this time."

A change came over Rod and before she realized what was happening, she was pushed up against the house with Rod's hand squeezing her throat. "I tried to do this the nice way." Rod's breath hit her in the face, he was that close. He slammed her head against the house once. "Now, let's go inside *our* house and talk so we can get this mess straightened out." He pulled her away, turned her and pushed her toward the door.

"You will not step foot inside *my* house, you piece of shit." Caroline stumbled to a stop and turned to face him, refusing to let him inside.

"Oh, and you think you can stop me." Rod laughed, then stopped suddenly, backhanding her across the face.

Caroline cried out, stumbled, but righted herself, straightening to face him again. "Yes," she vowed, and waited for the blow as he reared back his hand again, but the blow didn't come. She opened her eyes to see a familiar hand catch Rod's in mid strike before he was thrown over the railing and off the porch.

Jax stood in front of her, tilted her face up. His eyes went solid black; his fangs grew past his lips as a deep rumble came from his throat. He tilted her chin up higher to look at her neck. He used his thumb to wipe the blood from her nose and stared at the blood on his thumb. His head snapped around as an inhuman roar echoed around her. Then he was over the railing stalking after Rod, who was backpedaling away as his brother tried to help him up.

"Get away from me," Rod demanded, but it fell on deaf ears. Jax reached down, picking him up with one hand. His other hand wrapped around his throat and squeezed.

"Doesn't feel good, does it, motherfucker?" Jax hissed as Rod kicked and gasped, trying to breathe. "Guess you didn't learn your lesson the first time."

Fred took off to help his brother, but Blaze was ready and blocked him with his body like a linebacker. Fred flipped off his feet and lay flat on his back, moaning.

Caroline looked back to Rod, who was turning a pale shade of gray. She ran down the steps toward Jax. She felt a little dizzy, but she made it. "Jax, let him go," Caroline ordered, pulling on his arm. "I don't want you to get in trouble."

"Go inside, Caroline." Jax reared back and tossed Rod halfway across the yard. "Me and Rod are just going to have a little discussion."

Sid walked up, turning her toward the house, and Jax made his way toward Rod, who was trying to crawl away. "Go on, Caroline," Sid said, giving her a little push with a grin of anticipation. "I'll make sure he doesn't do anything he shouldn't."

Caroline was too busy walking toward the house watching Jax with a worried frown to see the grin of anticipation cross Sid's face.

******

Jax threw and kicked Rod all the way to the barn without saying a word, totally deaf to the pleading and crying Rod was doing. Once inside, Jax picked him up, slamming him on a stack of boxes.

Turning, Jax walked a few steps away to clear and calm his mind. Regaining control after seeing Caroline bloody and bruised was near impossible.

"Did I miss anything?" Sid walked in, his narrowed eyes zeroing in on Rod. "Guess not. He's still breathing and has his scalp."

"Oh, God." Rod started to move off the boxes, but Jax turned around and with only his glare, he stopped Rod cold.

"If you even attempt to escape, I will kill you before you realize it," Jax hissed, his fangs gleaming pure white.

"I swear I will never come near her again." Rod's body and voice shook with fear.

"Obviously you're a liar, because that is the same thing I heard the last time we had a visit." Jax's eyes narrowed dangerously.

"No, I'm not." Rod shook his head. "She called *me*. Wanted to talk and see what we could work out."

Jax didn't even react to that. He just stared at Rod. "Women in my tribe were held at the highest honor," Jax responded, his tone level. "I think I explained to you exactly what happens to abusers of women."

"Oh, you did, in great detail." Sid nodded, glancing at Rod with fake sympathy. "You sure as hell did."

"Do you remember?" Jax asked Rod, and when Rod didn't answer right away, Jax was in Rod's face, pulling his head back by the hair and holding a knife to Rod's throat. "I asked you a fucking question."

Rod swallowed hard, the knife at his throat scraping against his Adam's apple. "Ye...yes, I remember."

Jax pricked Rod's throat with the knife. "And still you laid a hand on her."

"I'd say since he has big enough balls to ignore your warning, you should cut them off and then scalp his dumb ass." Sid's eyes had also grown dark with anger.

"I didn't mean to, but she wouldn't let me in our house." Rod gulped, realizing what he'd just said. "Her house. She wouldn't let me in *her* house."

Jax pulled the knife away from his neck before punching him in the face, but not hard enough to knock him out. He wanted Rod awake for what was to come.

Knowing he had certain rules he had to follow, Jax figured he'd give Rod a fighting chance. Then he'd scalp the bastard and feed his carcass to the animals. Just like the old days, the old ways.

"Stand up." Jax sneered, but when Rod was too

slow, Sid picked him up, shoving him to his feet. "Take your best shot."

"Oh, shit." Sid grinned. "This is going to be good."

"What?" Rod stared from Jax to Sid, back to Jax again. "No, I'm not doing it."

"I'm giving you a fighting chance to live, you piece of shit, so I suggest you seize the moment before I change my mind." Jax looked him up and down. "Let's see just how hard you can hit, or am I not the right gender? Do you only hit women?"

Rod swung out, clipping Jax on the jaw, knocking his head to the side. Jax slowly turned his head toward Rod with a sinister smile, one that could turn the blood cold. "That's it? That's all you got?"

"You moved," Rod accused, his eyes shifting around nervously.

"No, no, he didn't." Sid shook his head. "You're just a pussy and hit like a little bitch."

Jax felt the heat of anger consume him. Rod's hit didn't faze him, but if he had hit Caroline that hard, which he surely had, Jax was beyond livid. His blood boiled at the thought. Pulling his knife back out of its sheath, he headed toward Rod. "Time to die, you son of a bitch."

Grabbing his hair in a punishing grip, Jax pulled Rod's head back, the knife at his scalp.

"Jax, no!" Caroline cried. "Please don't do this."

"Get in the house, Caroline," Jax ordered, his eyes still on Rod.

"Please, Caroline, please stop him." Rod cried and begged, his eyes pleading with Caroline.

Caroline walked up, getting into Rod's face. "This has nothing to do with you, asshole. You are going to definitely pay for what you did, but not at the expense of Jax," she spat, but then glanced up at Jax. "Please."

Blaze had followed, dragging Rod's brother with him. He shoved him next to Rod before glancing at Jax. "Sloan and the rest of them are on their way."

Jax glared at Blaze before his eyes met Caroline's. He cursed, pulling Rod away from them. He grabbed him around the throat again.

"Once again, you will live another day, but I am going to warn you now that no matter what happens with the human police or even the VC Council, we are not done." Jax hissed the words so only Rod could hear him. "She is mine and no one harms what's mine. I will find you when you least expect it and you will pay for what you did here today, do you understand me?"

Rod nodded, not looking relieved at all. In fact, he looked more scared, which was what Jax wanted.

"The only reason you continue to breathe at this moment is because of her, but she will not be around the next time, and there will be a next time." Jax let that warning hang in the air.

"Let him go, Jax." Sloan's voice echoed through the barn.

Jax didn't just let him go. He slung him toward Sloan.

"Jill, take Caroline inside," Sloan ordered, his eyes on Rod, who lay at his feet.

"Yes, sir." Jill grabbed Caroline's elbow, pulling her away, but Sloan stopped them.

Jax watched as Sloan inspected Caroline's swollen and bruised face and felt his rage. Sloan nodded, letting Caroline go with Jill. Once the women left, Sloan bent down, lifting Rod to his feet.

"I want you to take a good look around at each face." Sloan shoved Rod back. "Do it!"

Rod jumped at Sloan's bellow and did as he was told. Jax was the last he looked at before turning back to Sloan, but Sloan ignored him. "If you claim Caroline, I have the right to arrest and sentence this piece of shit under Council law," Sloan informed Jax.

"I claim her as mine." Jax didn't hesitate and received a nod of approval from every Warrior present.

"Then he will be arrested under Council law, but I will warn you"—Sloan grabbed Rod by the shirt front, pulling him close—"if you're released into human custody for any reason, do not think it's over. We are VC Warriors and we protect what's ours. You have harmed one of ours. Every face you have looked upon will hunt you down and bring you to our justice, as it was thousands of years ago, if the law fails. And we will be watching."

Every Warrior smashed their fist against their chest and chanted, their eyes promising Rod something worse than death itself and, even though he didn't understand them, the look in his eyes showed his full terror.

"Take him," Sloan told Damon and Duncan. "I'll be right behind you."

"What about him?" Jared pulled Fred up by his hair.

"Did you do anything to stop him?" Sloan asked the younger man, who shook his head, too afraid to speak. "Then you are just as guilty. Take him also."

Once everyone walked out of the barn, Jax and Sloan were the only ones left. "How did you not kill the son of a bitch?"

Jax took his eyes away from the group to look at Sloan. "Because she asked me not to."

"These women are going to make us pussies, my friend." Sloan actually clapped Jax on the back. "Now, go take care of Caroline, and I promise if I feel like the son of a bitch needs taking out, you'll have the honor."

"Agreed and much appreciated." Jax and Sloan walked out of the barn. Sid waited, leaning against the outside, looking as if he were pouting.

"Couldn't you have waited two more minutes before riding in to save the day?" Sid grumbled at Sloan. "He was this close to scalping the son of a bitch."

"Jesus." Sloan shook his head, walking away. "Sid, you need to calm the hell down. Can't Lana do anything to keep you on a tighter rope?"

"Oh, she can do plenty." Sid wiggled his eyebrows. "But I'm the one who's good with the ropes."

Jax ignored Sid as he made his way to the house. Once he saw Caroline's face and neck, he was going to want to kill the bastard all over again. Fuck, and did he really just claim her in front of the Warriors? A surprisingly satisfied grin took over his face at that thought. Yeah, he had claimed her without any hesitation whatsoever. Caroline Fitzpatrick was his and he didn't give a shit who knew it.

## Chapter 15

"Don't worry." Jill stood inside with Caroline, who was pacing back and forth. "Nothing is going to happen with Sloan there."

"I just don't want Jax to get in trouble over me." Caroline sighed, then touched her swollen cheek. "Does it look bad?"

"It looks sore." Jill grimaced. "He must have hit you pretty hard. Has he done this before?"

"Once. When I was in a trance, I heard how he was treating my sister. No one thought I knew what was going on, but I did. I just couldn't say anything to let them know. Before this I'd been blind to who he really was. I broke it off with him and kicked him out. When I was cleaning out the apartment, he showed up acting all crazy and hit me." Caroline jumped when the front door opened.

Slade walked in, looking at her face. "Are you having a lot of pain?" He reached out to tilt her face so he could see it better. The Warrior Slade was gone and in his place was Dr. Buchanan.

"It doesn't feel pleasant, but I'm okay." Caroline kept looking toward the door.

"It's over, Caroline." Slade smiled down at her. "He's talking to Sloan now and will be in shortly. Why don't you let me look closer to make sure nothing's cracked?"

"Okay. Where do you want me?" Caroline glanced one more time at the door, wishing Jax would return.

"Jump up on the counter there so I can see you under the light." Slade pointed toward the counter that not even two hours ago, Jax was…. Okay, on to safer thoughts.

Hoping her bruising hid her blush, she headed over and climbed up with Slade's help. Jill followed, ready if Slade needed any help. Before Slade could examine her, Jax walked in and headed straight toward her.

"Is she okay?" He frowned, staring at the side of her face.

"I don't know yet." Slade started his examination. The whole time, Caroline stared at Jax. Slade felt her face gently and then her throat. "I don't feel anything that could be broken, but without an X-ray, I wouldn't know if she had any fractures. How hard did he hit you?"

Okay, she didn't want to answer that with Jax standing there. If he knew, he would probably go back out there and kill Rod. Not that he didn't deserve it, but Jax had too much going for him to kill someone over this.

"Answer him, Caroline," Jax demanded with a

frown.

"I don't know," Caroline replied. "I mean, that's kind of a hard question to answer."

"No, really it's not." Slade frowned. "Did he hit you with his fist or…?"

"No, he backhanded me," she replied, keeping her eyes off Jax and on Slade. Now that it was over, her tears threatened to break free. She didn't want to be a big baby in front of all these tough, strong fighters. She wanted to belong, and weak crybabies didn't belong.

"Did it snap your head back? Did you see flashes of light, pinpoints of lights like stars, or did you get nauseous?" Slade asked, his frown growing as he watched her expression.

"Yes," she replied, her lip trembling.

"To which one?" Slade asked, then cursed when she just looked at them. "Does your neck hurt when I move it?"

She relaxed, letting Slade move her neck around. "No, not really." Her eyes did meet Jax's hardened gaze as he watched.

"It's a yes or no question, Caroline," Slade replied, his doctor voice in full control.

"No," she answered immediately, and then figured she'd better come clean. "But I do have a headache and I keep getting dizzy."

"You probably have a concussion." Slade looked over at Jill. "Can you get my penlight? It looks just like a flashlight, but much smaller."

Jill nodded, taking off out the door. She was back in seconds, digging in his bag for a little penlight.

"That was fast." Caroline smiled, but immediately grimaced when it hurt her cheek.

"She's one hell of an assistant." Slade winked at Jill, who grinned proudly.

"I'm a better Warrior though." Her beaming grin turned into a frown when Slade rolled his eyes. "You just want me to quit and be your full-time assistant. That so is not happening, Buchanan."

Slade smiled at Caroline before checking her eyes. "Looks like you have a concussion." Slade turned the penlight off, then turned to Jax. "She really should be seen and have her cheek as well as eye socket X-rayed. I can meet you at the hospital."

"No, I'll be fine." Caroline slowly slid off the counter, but her equilibrium was off and she stumbled as a wave of dizziness overwhelmed her. Jax grabbed her, holding her close.

"What if she took some of my blood?" Jax asked

without looking at Caroline. "Would that be safe for her and would it take care of the concussion or any fractures she may have?"

"It definitely would and it wouldn't take much. Nothing is displaced so it wouldn't heal wrong, that much I can tell." Slade nodded. "You claimed her so you have that right. If you do give her the blood, someone will still have to keep an eye on her for a few hours. If she goes to sleep, she should be woken up every half an hour. If you find it hard to wake her up, then you need to call me or get her to the nearest emergency room as soon as possible."

"Claimed me?" Surprise flickered through Caroline, though she didn't know exactly what that meant.

Jax ignored her question as he stuck his hand out, shaking Slade's hand. "Thanks."

"No problem." Slade made to grab his bag, but Jill already had it. "Make sure to call me if anything changes."

"We can stay if you want us to," Jill offered, and Slade nodded in agreement.

"We'll be fine," Jax assured them. "But thanks."

Sid and Sloan walked in as Slade and Jill left. "You okay?" Sloan frowned, staring at her swollen face.

"I'm good," Caroline lied. "What's going to happen to him?"

Everyone knew exactly who she was talking about, but it was Sid who answered. "Well, right now Jared is recounting Damon's beheading skills, while Damon sits in the backseat next to the bastard." Sid grinned. "He may not survive the ride to be booked because it looks like he's about ready to have a stroke, he's so scared."

"He'll be taken care of." Sloan gave her the answer to what she was really asking, but he didn't go into detail. "We can promise you that you will never have to deal with him again."

Caroline nodded. No longer able to ignore the shaking in her hands spreading to the rest of her body, she needed to have a moment to herself. "Excuse me. I'll be right back." She headed quickly to the bathroom and closed the door behind her.

Touching her throbbing cheek, she slowly made her way to the mirror. Her appearance shocked her. Swollen and bruised from her jawline to her eye, she'd known her vision was getting funky in her right eye and now she understood why; it was almost swollen shut. She lifted her chin to see what that looked like and gasped at the bruising around her neck from Rod's fingers.

Swallowing hard, she tried to keep the sobs away, but the more she looked at herself, the more upset she became. She had been so wrong about Rod and that scared her. Actually, Rod's craziness from moments earlier terrified her to the point she felt like she was losing it. Tears rolled down her face, dripping from her trembling chin.

She barely heard the knock on the bathroom door, but her throat was so tight with tears, she couldn't respond.

"Caroline?" Jax knocked again as he opened the door.

She couldn't look at him, didn't want him to see her weakness and fear. She wanted to be strong for him, but was failing miserably. He appeared behind her. His eyes locked onto hers in the mirror before he turned her around and took her into his arms.

"You should have let me kill him," Jax whispered into her hair. "But I will promise you this, he will never hurt you again."

"I couldn't let you kill someone over me." Caroline sniffed, her tears slowing. "He's not worth it."

"But you are." Jax pulled her away to look down into her bruised face. "Never doubt that."

"I can't stop shaking." Caroline rubbed her hands up and down her arms.

Jax picked her up and carried her out of the bathroom and into her bedroom, laying her gently on the bed. "If you take some of my blood, you will heal quickly." Jax tilted her chin, his gaze going to her face and neck. Anger darkened his eyes.

"You would do that for me"?" Caroline touched his hand. "Lana said that is reserved for mates."

"I claimed you as mine in front of my brothers," Jax replied, his eyes never leaving hers. There was no hesitation in his voice. "We will not do the mating ceremony, but you are mine, Caroline. My blood is your blood."

"Please don't be saying this because you feel sorry for me." Caroline frowned, her eyes feeling heavy.

"Hey." He shook her gently. "Stay with me."

"I am." She opened her eyes wide; well, at least her uninjured eye opened wide.

"And I never say anything I don't mean." Jax moved a strand of hair off her face. "I think you should know that about me by now."

"I do." Caroline's eye drooped slowly.

"Caroline, you need to stay awake." Jax grasped her arm, pulling her up gently.

"I am, but I just feel really sleepy." Caroline tried to focus on Jax, but she could hardly keep her eyes open. "My face really hurts. Can't you just wake me up in half an hour? I think I'll be okay."

"Fuck this." Jax used his fangs to puncture his wrist and then moved it toward her mouth. "Take my blood, Caroline. I can't stand to see you in pain."

Caroline placed her lips against his wrist. The first taste of his blood was a shock. It was warm and had a spicy metallic taste. It wasn't unpleasant, but it was foreign to her taste buds. Yet the more she took, the more she wanted.

"That's good, babe." He pulled his arm away.

"Can I lie down now?" Caroline asked, but instead, she crawled up onto his lap, rested her head on his chest, and that was all she remembered.

# Chapter 16

Jax lay with Caroline in his arms all night, waking her every half hour. He watched as the swelling and bruising faded from her face. She was almost completely healed.

He had never shared his blood with anyone. The woman in his arms was the only person, human or vampire, who had his blood running through her. His protectiveness for her was overwhelming. He would have killed for her yesterday, but her words had stopped him. Only her words.

She moved restlessly, indicating she was trying to wake up. He held her closer, breathing in her scent. It had been a night of firsts for him because he had never lain in a bed with a woman he'd had sex with. In truth, he had never lain in bed with a woman in his arms until that moment.

Her eyes fluttered open, closed, and then fluttered open again. He knew when she realized she was in bed with him, but instead of pulling away, she snuggled closer, holding him tighter. He didn't want this to end. He could lie with her for days, even weeks, holding her, and that threw him a little.

"How you feeling?" He watched her closely.

Her head tilted slightly so she could look up at him. Her hand slowly reached for his face. "Better." Her voice was husky with sleep. "I think."

"The swelling and bruising is almost gone." He wasn't for sure about her neck because he couldn't see it, but he knew without a doubt that was healing also.

Slowly she sat up, getting her bearings. "That's amazing." She gently felt and poked at her cheek. "It doesn't even hurt."

"You still have a headache?" He tilted her chin up so he could see her neck.

"No, not at all," she said, surprised, then leaned in and kissed his cheek. "Thank you, Jax."

"For what?" He frowned, feeling uncomfortable. He didn't get many thank-yous and didn't know exactly how to say "'you're welcome.'"

Caroline's eyes widened slightly. "Well, you got a minute, because the list is quite long?" She smiled before reaching out and wrapping her arms around his neck to give him a long hug. "I'll just say for everything, and leave it at that. Obviously, you don't like thank-yous or praise. So, I won't make you uncomfortable."

"And that's why I l—" What the fuck was happening to him? He didn't know what the hell love was so no way in hell was it going to be spewing from his mouth.

"Why you what?" Caroline tilted her head to stare at him.

Jax didn't know what in the hell to say. They just sat staring at each other. Quickly, he pulled himself out from under her and stood. "Why don't you…?" Jax ran his hand through his hair. "Do what you do in the morning and I'll go start some coffee?"

"Ah, okay." Caroline looked at him, confused, as she swung her feet over the side of the bed.

Staying close, he watched as she slowly stood, stretched, and took a step. "You still feel dizzy?" He wouldn't leave her until he was sure she was okay, even though he wanted to run like hell out of the room.

She turned to give him a bright smile. "Actually, I feel amazing." She took a few steps and then stopped. "You should bottle that stuff up, Jax. You could make a fortune. I feel like a million bucks. You think I can have a sip every once in a while as a pick-me-up?" she teased.

Jax actually laughed, momentarily forgetting that he'd almost said the word he didn't even think was in his vocabulary.

"At a low cost, I think we could work something out." He winked at her, making sure she was okay before heading downstairs. Caroline was turning his world upside down and he actually felt pretty good about it. Yeah, the world had to be fucking ending or some shit. There were too many 'firsts' happening to him in the span of a few hours, and even though he felt good, maybe even happy, he had a strong feeling that wouldn't last. Something big was coming, it always did.

******

Caroline had showered, dressed, stared at her face in complete awe and was now sitting across from Jax, drinking coffee and enjoying his company. She couldn't believe he had stayed and held her all night. She remembered each time he had gently woken her, asked her questions before allowing her to go back to sleep. And then that morning, she was almost sure he had come close to saying he loved her. She'd debated with herself as she showered, and even as she sat directly across from him, whether that was what he was going to say before he'd abruptly cut himself off.

Honestly, it didn't matter. If he didn't say the words she felt, she could live with that... she hoped.

"What happened yesterday?" Jax interrupted her musing with something she definitely didn't want to talk about, but the look on his face told her that was exactly what they were going to do.

"I was painting and thought I heard someone on the porch." Caroline frowned, remembering her shock at opening the door to find Rod standing directly in front of her.

"And you opened the door without asking who it was?" Jax guessed correctly.

"I didn't even know if anyone was out there," she defended herself. By his narrowed gaze, she knew he was not happy. "So yes, I opened the door and Rod was standing there with his brother in the yard."

"Go on." Jax took a drink of coffee, watching her closely over the rim.

"I asked him what he was doing there." Her hand shook as she brought her coffee cup to her lips. "Is this really necessary? It's over."

"It is." Jax frowned. "And it's far from over."

"What do you mean, it's far from over?" She set her coffee down before she sloshed the hot liquid all over her.

"Stop changing the subject." Jax eyed her knowingly.

"It's still the same subject," Caroline hedged. "How am I changing the subject?"

"What did he say, Caroline?" Jax was no fool and knew exactly what she was doing.

"He said he was there to take me back. He had given me time to realize my mistake." Her voice trembled. "I told him that he made a mistake coming here and to get off my property. That's when he grabbed me by the throat and slammed me against the house."

"When did he hit you?" Jax's voice had changed and so had his eyes. They were black instead of their usual beautiful gold.

"He said he wanted to see our house, but I refused to let him in." Caroline looked away from Jax. "And he hit me. You know the rest."

Jax sat, saying nothing for a long time. She became fidgety and uncomfortable under his stare, to the point she got up and poured more coffee for herself before sitting back down. She sensed his eyes on her the whole time.

"Jax, can we please talk about something else?" She finally broke the silence. "I don't want you to be upset with me."

"I'm not upset with you." He finally spoke. "I'm trying to keep myself from leaving and killing the son of a bitch."

"Oh, well, I don't want you doing that either. It's not worth it."

Jax gave a sinister laugh. "Yes, it would be totally worth it." As quickly as he laughed, his face changed. "He will never lay a hand on you again. That I can promise you."

Caroline could only nod because she was afraid if she opened her mouth, the sobs she was holding back would escape, and she was so over crying. After a few minutes of more silence, she felt it was safe to speak without blubbering. "So what are your plans for today?" She tried for a normal conversation.

"I was supposed to start the training program, but Sloan let me off." Jax got up to put his cup in the sink. "He really cares for you."

"Who? Sloan?" Caroline shrugged. "He has to. My sister is married to one of his Warriors." She laughed.

"No, that's not it," Jax added, but then dropped it. "Blaze and Sid can get things started."

Okay, this conversation was strange. Was he bringing up Sloan liking her for a reason? When he turned and wouldn't meet her gaze, she knew. Call it women's intuition.

"I don't have feelings for Sloan Murphy." By the flash of relief that disappeared a split second later, she knew she had been right. She also knew not to dwell on it because that wasn't the kind of man Jax was. He threw something out there, wanting to know without actually asking. She understood it, answered it, and would leave it at that. It also made her heart skip a beat to even imagine he was jealous, but she wouldn't use that to her advantage.

The only reply he gave was a nod, without meeting her gaze.

"And please don't change anything because of me.

I'll be fine. Go do your training, Jax." Caroline hated to be a nuisance to anyone. "I have so much to do with school starting next week."

"Next week?" That got his attention. "Adam said it doesn't start for two weeks."

"No, we're starting a week early because of snow days." She frowned. "And why does that matter?"

Jax didn't answer her right away; instead, he pulled out his phone and typed a text. Actually, he didn't look like he was planning on answering her at all.

"What's going on?" Caroline pushed. "Why does it matter when school starts?"

"We're going to plant Adam, Steve, and Jill in your classroom," Jax answered with a tone that indicated it was a done deal.

"They can't do that." Caroline frowned. "Is this because—"

"They are doing it and yes, it is because of Mika," Jax cut her off. "None of the women are being left alone."

"Jill is a woman. Isn't that putting her in danger?" Caroline didn't like this idea at all. "And isn't that spreading you guys thin? I know how busy you are."

His eyes shot to hers. "Jill is a Warrior and a damn

good one at that." Something flickered in his eyes before it was gone. "And our women will not be left unguarded in the face of danger. It's a done deal, Caroline."

A terrible thought occurred to her. "Am I putting my kids in danger by teaching them?" Caroline gasped.

Jax didn't answer right away, but when he did, there was a fierceness to his voice. "We won't let anything happen to you or the kids." Then he added, "This is a precaution. Trust me."

Caroline stood and walked toward Jax, putting her arms around him. "I do trust you." She did trust him, with all her heart.

## Chapter 17

As Jax walked into the warehouse, his mind was elsewhere. He had dropped Caroline off at the compound. She had insisted yesterday that he go to training, but he'd flatly refused. He hadn't been ready to leave her alone yet and still felt that way, but he had responsibilities.

The workout area was full. He walked through, making his way toward Blaze and Sid. Everyone stared, but got out of his way. He spotted Katrina sitting alone. From what he could tell, she was the only female in the group. She was quiet and kept to herself. He didn't know much about her, but that would soon change.

Sid had filled him in on the phone about how the first session had gone. They'd mainly gone over rules and what was expected—to get ready for an ass kicking they'd never forget—and then did some hardcore conditioning.

"Well, we lost ten already." Sid grinned when Jax stopped in front of them. "And after tonight, I expect to lose a few more."

"Is Katrina the only female?" Jax once again glanced her way, then surveyed the rest of the group, which was sizing him up.

"Yeah, and she looks a nervous wreck, but she's a determined little thing." Sid nodded in her direction.

"So you say we lost ten so far?" Jax cocked an eyebrow when Sid's grin widened with a nod. "Okay, let's see how many more pussies we can flush out today."

"Even though you stabbed me, I can't help but like your Native American ass." Sid followed Jax to the middle of the mats, with Blaze right behind them.

"I'm Jax Wheeler." Jax's voice boomed through the warehouse. The low rumble of conversation stopped at his first word. "Looking at you, I can tell if you are VC Warrior material and right now, I can tell you half of you will be running out of this room crying like bitches."

Jax paused for effect.

"I'm not here to hold your hand. I'm not your friend. I'm training you to keep order and possibly save lives. I take my job seriously and if for one minute I feel you're not right for this job, I will personally escort you off this mat and out the door." Jax's eyes narrowed, seeing one of the larger candidates roll his eyes. Without saying a word, he walked over to stand in front of him. "You got a problem with your eyes?"

The large candidate looked around at the others who seemed to fade away from him. "No." Even though he said one word, it sounded cocky.

"No, sir." Jax's voice was deadly.

The guy hesitated. "No, sir," he repeated, not sounding at all like he meant it.

An audible gasp filled the room when Jax punched the guy in the eye. "Now you do." Jax growled. "Get the fuck off my mats and out of my building."

Jax heard a few "holy shits," Sid's included, as well as mumblings. "Anyone else?" Jax took the time to look each candidate in the eye before turning toward Blaze. "Get them running and warmed up."

Blaze was grinning from ear to ear, but at Jax's order, the smile disappeared. "You heard him," Blaze shouted. "Get your asses moving!"

"Bad day?" Sid laughed, following Jax off the mat.

"Not at all." Jax leaned against the wall, crossing his arms across his chest, watching each candidate run. "Just don't like cocky bastards."

\*\*\*\*\*\*

At the compound, Caroline sat in the kitchen staring at her laptop. She hadn't argued with Jax when he said no one was available to come to her house and that he would have to take her to the compound. She had work to do, getting her class schedules and planners ready, which she could do anywhere with her laptop.

Yesterday, after their little talk, they'd enjoyed the rest of the day and Jax had actually helped her finish painting the living room. Their teasing paint fight turned into a sex marathon, but only after Jax made sure, after repeated questioning, that she felt okay.

"Give me your damn phone." Lana walked in, a pissed expression on her face.

"Well, hello to you too." Caroline frowned, but dug into her purse trying to find her phone. Finally feeling it with her hand, she pulled it out and handed it to her sister. She watched wide-eyed as Lana checked it and then shoved the phone at her.

"Twenty-five missed calls and just as many text messages, all unanswered and unchecked." Lana put her hands on her hips. "Why do you even have a phone, Caroline?"

"I'm sorry, but I figured Sid would tell you I was okay." Caroline tossed her phone back in her purse.

"Yeah, well, he did, but dammit, answer your damn phone or at least check it," Lana scolded. Concern etched her features as she sat down, staring at her face. "Sid said your face was really bad, but it's not really even swollen."

Caroline blushed, self-consciously touching her cheek.

Lana frowned until understanding crossed her face. "No!" Her mouth opened wide. "Jax gave you his blood? You're mated to Jax Wheeler?"

"Oh, no!" Caroline shook her head, setting her sister straight. "He just let me have some to help me heal."

"What exactly is going on with the two of you?" Lana narrowed her eyes.

"Lana, can you please stop being a cop for one second and just be my sister?" Caroline sighed. "I get so tired of being interrogated by you."

"Ah, excuse me, I am being your sister and want to know what's going on between you and Jax," Lana grumbled.

"Whatever." Caroline rolled her eyes before turning her attention back to her laptop.

"Okay, then how's this?" Lana said. Flipping her hair, she leaned close to Caroline. "Oh, my God, have you and Jax… you know… done it?"

"What?" Caroline moved back, looking at Lana as if she'd lost her mind.

"Does he have a big one?" Lana giggled, pointing down to her lap. "You know… did it fit and stuff?"

"That's exactly what we'd like to know." Nicole walked in and sat down, with Tessa following. "And why in the hell are you talking like a valley girl?"

"Because she has lead poisoning from all the bullets she plays with." Caroline was still staring at her sister.

"No, I asked Caroline a simple question and she thought I was playing cop with her." Lana switched back to her regular voice. "She wanted sister-talk, so I gave her sister-talk."

"We never ever talked like that." Caroline chuckled, shaking her head while still staring at her sister.

"Thank God, 'cause I really like you both and would hate to have to kill you." Nicole gave them both a teasing grin. She then turned serious. "Now back to the question." Nicole looked directly at Caroline.

"What question?" Caroline asked, confused.

"Does Jax Wheeler have a big one?" Nicole leaned forward, as did Tessa and Lana, to hear the answer to that question.

The seriousness in Nicole's voice as well as the looks on their faces was hilarious and Caroline burst out laughing. "You guys are so not right."

Soon they were all laughing, with Nicole, Tessa, and Lana comparing their men, but Caroline kept her mouth shut, except to laugh. Jax Wheeler was not something she was willing to share with other women, even if it was just talk.

Before any of them goaded her into joining in, Jill burst into the room with a look of horror on her face.

"What's wrong?" all the women shouted at the same time, except for Caroline. New to the Warrior way, she didn't totally understand the dangers they faced, or the worry the women suffered each time their men were out in the field.

"I'm a dead woman." Jill held papers to her chest. "That's what's wrong."

"What did you do now?" Nicole grinned. It was common knowledge that Jill had a knack for getting herself into messes.

"You know that ad I asked you to place in the paper?" She looked at Nicole.

"For the open secretary job for Sloan, Thursday." Nicole nodded. "Did I mess it up?"

"No, kind of the opposite." Jill slapped the papers down on the table. "The ad did so well we have over a hundred women signed up for interviews."

## Chapter 18

After Jax picked Caroline up from the compound, they rode home in silence. Her phone kept dinging, but she ignored it. She really was bad for that.

"Who's trying to get ahold of you?" Jax asked, keeping his eyes on the road.

Caroline frowned and dug for her phone. Clicking it on, she sighed. "It's just my friend who teaches with me. They're meeting for dinner and drinks tonight and want me to come. It's just something we do before the school year starts."

"Do you want to go?" This time Jax did look her way.

"No, not really." Caroline hesitated. She kind of did and yet she didn't. "It will be too much of a hassle."

Jax pulled into her drive, down the driveway and parked. He hadn't responded, his attention checking out the area around her house. Once inside, he dropped his guard just a little.

"What time are they meeting and where?" Jax asked, glancing at his watch.

"About eight at the Mansion Hill Tavern," she replied, setting her stuff on the kitchen table. "Jax, it's okay. I know you have better things to do than run me everywhere. I've got work to do anyway, as I'm sure you do."

He was in front of her, grabbing her to force her to look at him. "You have an hour to get ready." Jax turned her, gently pushing her toward the steps.

She turned back toward him. "But—" He stopped her from arguing with a kiss that not only made her forget what she was arguing, but damn near made her forget her name.

His lips left hers as he turned her again, giving her a sharp smack on the ass, sending her to get ready. She wondered if she tried to argue again would he kiss her one more time, but instead, she headed up the stairs and into her room.

She had no clue what she was going to wear and was thankful she had already unpacked and put all her clothes away. At least that was one thing she had completely marked off her long list, she thought as she looked around at all the unpacked boxes stacked everywhere. Selecting her pale yellow sundress and a pair of her many summer sandals, she laid them on the bed before heading to the bathroom to shower.

Within half an hour, Caroline was ready and stood in front of the mirror staring at herself as she gave her hair one last fluff and checked her makeup one last time. She knew she took a little extra effort for Jax. Usually, she wore minimal makeup, but tonight she added just a little more. So far Jax had only seen her in jeans and T-shirts and, well, naked. Yeah, she dressed specifically for him tonight.

With a sigh and a shrug, she headed downstairs. Jax was sitting at the kitchen table, texting. He glanced up at her for a split second, then back to his phone before his eyes slowly came back to her.

"You seriously think I'm going to let you out of this house wearing that dress?" His eyes narrowed dangerously.

"What's wrong with my dress?" Caroline frowned, looking down at herself.

"Absolutely nothing." Jax stood, his eyes staring at her breasts. "It's what's in the dress that's the problem. It shows every damn curve I've kissed, touched, and licked."

"But I love this dress." Caroline actually pouted. She was going to play this one because she really didn't want to change.

"Oh, so do I, but behind closed doors." Jax turned her around, his hand running down her ass. "Yeah, not happening. Go change."

"Please, Jax." Caroline tried the pout again, but it didn't look like it was going to work and she really hated to resort to it anyway. "I don't have anything else to wear," she lied. She had plenty to wear, but knowing he liked her in this dress, she wanted to wear it more than ever.

"I don't believe that for one minute." Jax turned her around and flicked his thumb across her nipple, making her moan. Her nipple puckered, sticking out underneath the material. "Jesus, you're going to get someone killed, because if one son of a bitch touches you, I will kill him."

"No one will touch me, Jax." Caroline chuckled. "Most men don't even pay me any attention. You'll see you have nothing to worry about and no killings need to take place."

Jax frowned and opened the door, following her out, his eyes sliding down her body. "Are you wearing anything under that dress?"

"Maybe." Caroline gave him a sly smile over her shoulder.

"Jesus." Jax squeezed his eyes shut, giving his head a hard shake. "This is going to be a long night."

\*\*\*\*\*\*

Jax found a place at the bar where he had a clear line of vision to Caroline. And she had been dead wrong. There may be a killing, because every male eye in the place followed her as she made her way to her friends.

"Hey, Jax." The bartender walked up. "What brings you in tonight?"

"Not much." Jax didn't feel the need to explain.

"How you doing, Tony?"

"Can't complain," he replied and then laughed. "Still kickin'. What can I get you tonight?"

Jax's keen hearing picked up Caroline's laugh. His eyes swung her way and just her smile alone made him feel things he'd never felt.

"Just a beer." He looked back at Tony. He wanted something way stronger, but needed to make sure he was clearheaded. It took a lot to get a vampire drunk and usually hard liquor did it.

Sitting alone, Jax focused on who was in the bar, who left the bar, and who entered. Anyone who even looked his way he studied, knowing his brother could be here, be anyone, and he wouldn't even know it. That was what made Mika so dangerous, and the fact pissed him off. He hated feeling helpless to the whims of his lunatic brother.

"Hey." A woman in a tight red dress slid next to him at the bar. "Buy a girl a drink."

"No." Jax didn't hesitate, his glare told her to get lost. He didn't want to be rude. Ah, hell, who was he kidding? He was rude, but he couldn't lose focus and the only woman he wanted to buy anything for sat across the room staring at him.

"Jerk," the woman hissed at him before moving away.

"Making friends again?" Tony laughed, shaking his head.

"Always." Jax tipped his beer at him with a grin.

The later it got, the busier the bar became. Jax had no trouble keeping his sights on Caroline. Each time someone stood in his way, Jax glared at them until they moved, which was pretty damn quick. Jax was a huge man and hard to miss. A few times he sneered at them, showing his fangs, but mostly his size and glare had them scurrying away.

He became alert when Caroline stood and headed his way. A low growl played in his throat as men turned to watch her walk past. She stopped in front of him.

"You're wrong." Jax stared at her from his seated position at the bar.

"About what?" The smile she wore turned into a frown.

"Most men definitely notice you." Jax growled, his eyes leaving hers to glare at a few who continued to stare. "You finished before I kill someone?"

Caroline laughed. "Stop it." She touched his arm. "And yes, I'm ready to go, but my friends want to meet you."

"Caroline, I'm not a good people-meeter type of guy." Jax sat back on the bar stool, staring at her.

"Come on and loosen up." She giggled. "And meeter is not a word."

"It is a word because I just said it," Jax argued, then eyed her. "Are you drunk?"

"Nooo." She grinned, shaking her head. "I mean, I had a few drinks. I'm not a big drinker so it doesn't take much. I just feel a little….tingly."

Jax's head fell back as he laughed. When he looked back at her, his eyes went directly to her breasts, which were almost in his face. Her nipples were hard and begging for attention. Jax's laugh turned into a low growl. "Let's go meet your friends so I can show you exactly what tingly is."

"Mmmm, I can't wait." Caroline grabbed his hand and led him across the bar.

Jax lost count of how many times he called a guy a motherfucker, threatened and damn near killed someone openly staring at Caroline's luscious breasts. By the time they were at the table, he was in a mood that didn't suit a table full of schoolteachers.

"This is Jax Wheeler," Caroline introduced proudly. "This is Rachel, Donna, Erin, and Angie."

"Did you see those tits on her?" a man behind them was saying to his buddies. "Yellow is definitely my favorite color. I might need to go rub one off in the bathroom. Hell, if I'm lucky, she'll go in with me and do it her…."

Jax watched Caroline's face pale before it turned bright red. The rest of the women shifted uncomfortably as they tried to ignore the remarks.

"Nice to meet you, ladies." Jax nodded, then moved Caroline out of the way. "Now if you'll excuse me."

"Jax, please," Caroline whispered as she grabbed his arm stopping him. "It's really okay. We're leaving anyway."

"I'll be nice. Stay here with your friends." Jax gave her an unpleasant smile before he turned, grabbed the guy by the back of the neck and headed out of the bar. He would make sure the asshole understood what it meant to respect a lady.

Once in the parking lot, Jax released the guy with a hard shove. A crowd was already gathering and Jax knew he had to be careful. He was a VC Warrior and couldn't just go beating up assholes who didn't know how to respect a woman, so he had to get the crowd on his side.

"What the fuck!" The man turned to head toward Jax, but stopped after getting a better look at him.

"The *fuck* is"—Jax narrowed his eyes, his lip curled in a sneer—"you were talking about my lady."

The guy looked behind Jax, his courage seeming to grow a bit. "Yeah, well, what are you going to do about it?"

Jax actually laughed before lashing out, punching the guy in the mouth. "That for starters." Jax had turned himself so his back wasn't toward the guy's four friends.

The guy didn't look so cocky as he spat his own blood. "There are five of us." He tried to sound badass, but failed terribly when his voice trembled as his bloody lips began to swell.

"Good," Jax replied without blinking. His golden eyes darkened, ready for what was to come. When no one made a move toward him, Jax tilted his head. "I'm waiting."

"I don't want any trouble," one of the four said, raising his hands.

"You didn't feel that way when your friend here was running his mouth." Jax narrowed his eyes at him. "Where I come from a woman is treated with respect, and a man would have stepped in, which you didn't. So in my mind, that warrants an ass kicking."

A few male spectators who stood around mumbled their agreement. The women in the growing crowd were more vocal, shouting out "'hell yeah'" and "'damn straight.'"

"Fuck you, man." A different one of the four took off his shirt, showing a toned, muscled body. "He's right. There're five of us and one of you. The only ass kicking around here is going to be us kicking

*The Protectors - Jax*

your ass."

Jax cocked an eyebrow. "Well, I wish to fuck you'd hurry and get that done because I'm already bored with this fucking conversation."

Jax didn't hesitate. As soon as the muscled asshole made a move, Jax was all over him while fending off the other four. A few of the men standing around tried to help Jax, but he didn't need their help.

Within seconds, all five of the men lay on the ground bleeding and moaning. Jax reached down and grabbed the mouthy one by the front of the shirt, hauling him to his feet where they were nose to nose, well, to be correct, nose to broken nose.

"Listen and listen good. You and your friends are going to apologize to my lady and her friends at the table," Jax hissed, loud enough for them to hear over their moaning and the excitement of the crowd they had drawn. "And it better be good or we will end up back here, and if we end up back here, not one of you motherfuckers is going to be walking away. You understand me?" To make his point final, he made sure they each saw his fangs gleaming in the parking lot lights.

"I'm sorry... I didn't..." The guy didn't even try to hide his fear now as he stuttered his apology.

"Good, you're practicing, but save it until you're in front of the ladies, and you better make it good." Jax watched the others get their feet. "Now straighten up

*183*

and wipe some of the blood off. I promised I'd be nice and don't want to upset the ladies."

The crowd laughed outright when the five men tried to do as Jax said. As they walked back inside Jax nodded to a few guys who had tried to help him. The bar became quiet as the five, followed by Jax, walked into the bar toward Caroline and the women.

Jax stood back, listening closely as each and every one of the five men apologized to Caroline and her friends. When the guy who had been running his mouth finished his apology, he turned to look at Jax. He only gave the man a dismissive nod and watched as he and his friends walked away and out of the bar.

"That was pretty impressive." One of the woman at the table, he believed it was Rachel, smiled up at him. "Thank you."

"You're welcome," Jax replied, smiling at the group before turning to Caroline. He leaned close and whispered, "See, I was nice, only minimal bloodshed."

Caroline shook her head, a smile tugging at her lips. "One of them was missing his front tooth."

"You ready?" He grabbed her hand, ignoring her observation, then smiled at the women. "Have a nice evening, and if you need to, ask Tony to see you to your cars."

Funny how kicking someone's ass got around in a bar so quickly because not one man looked Caroline's way as they left. "See ya, Tony," Jax called out. "Make sure the ladies at the back table make it to their cars safely."

"You got it, Jax," Tony called out.

"You know him?" Caroline was trying to see over her shoulder who Jax was talking to.

"Honey, I know everybody." Jax protectively ushered her out the door.

## Chapter 19

Caroline walked downstairs feeling like crap. She didn't drink often, but when she did have a few, the next day she paid for it. Jax stood at the kitchen counter staring at her over the brim of his coffee cup. Heat immediately bloomed through her body, landing on her cheeks. She had been a total slut last night.

"Good morning." Jax's eyes crinkled at the corners. The cup hid his mouth, yet she knew he was smiling. "How you feeling?"

"Honestly, like a big pile of dog crap." She poured herself a cup of coffee. "Guess I drank more than I thought. I'm kind of a lightweight and don't drink often."

"What exactly did you drink?" Jax set his coffee cup on the counter, crossing his arms across his chest.

"Ice tea something." Caroline took a sniff of her coffee, closing her eyes in pleasure. "You could hardly taste any alcohol at all so it was perfect for me."

Jax chuckled, shaking his head. "Long Island Iced Tea, and that has five different liquors in it."

"Are you serious?" Caroline's eyes widened. "Well, they sure were good. I hardly tasted any alcohol."

"They? You had more than one?" Jax grinned. "Hell,

no wonder you were..."

When he trailed off, she looked up at him. "I acted like a slut, didn't I?" She sat down heavily at the kitchen table, putting her face in her hands.

"Hey." Jax walked over, pulling her hands away from her face. "Did you enjoy what we did last night?"

Caroline bit her lip and nodded. "Yes, I did." She then grinned. "Very much."

"So did I, and any time you want to do a striptease for me again, please, by all means...." Jax chuckled when she buried her face in her hands again. "You were amazing."

Loud pounding had Caroline putting her palms over her ears. "Make it stop." She moaned.

"Stay here," Jax ordered, all chuckling and smiling coming to a halt.

Caroline turned to see Jax open the door. "We need you guys." Lana walked past Jax, Sid following.

"Why, what's going on?" Caroline stood and grabbed the aspirin from a cabinet, downing three of them with a glass of water.

"You know that special project Jill set up?" Lana frowned, looking at Caroline closely. "What's wrong with you? You look like shit?"

"Oh, well, thank you." Caroline rolled her eyes. "I had a little too much to drink last night and—"

"But you're a lightweight and can't handle your liquor." Lana pointed out the obvious before turning toward Jax. "Why the hell are you letting my sister drink?"

"First of all, she's an adult who doesn't need you telling her what she can and cannot handle," Jax responded, his tone indicating he did not like being chastised by Lana. "And she was well taken care of." Jax then winked at Caroline, making her cheeks heat.

"Now, if you're finished getting on my nerves"— Caroline glared at Lana—"tell me what's going on."

"Oh, and she also gets bitchy the day after." Lana shot back with a glare of her own.

"Think we're going to see some sister-on-sister action?" Sid whispered to Jax, but loud enough to be heard.

"Shut up, Sid," both women growled. Caroline picked up and threw a dishrag at him and then grabbed her aching head.

Lana's phone dinged. Looking down, she cursed. "Come on and get dressed. We have to get to the warehouse."

"Why?" Caroline didn't want to get dressed. She wanted to lie around all day and not move unless it was to.... Her eyes met Jax's and his eyes darkened as if he could read her mind. Was he reading her mind?

"They had to move the interviews for Sloan's secretary to the warehouse because more women showed up without even applying." Lana shook her head. "Jill is in way over her head on this one and she's freaking out."

"How many women are we talking about?" Jax glanced at Sid.

"Hundreds at last count," Lana answered for Sid. "They need crowd control."

"Give me about ten minutes to get dressed." Caroline headed for the stairs. "This is something I need to see. Does Sloan know yet?"

"Not yet, but I'm sure he will very soon," Lana called after her. "Hurry up!"

******

Caroline loved riding on the back of Jax's motorcycle, except he made her wear a helmet. Even though she was a little sore from their previous night's activities, a grin spread across her face as she held on to Jax tighter. He knew she liked to go fast, so when it was clear, he sped them down the road.

Too soon he was pulling into a parking lot that was packed with cars. Women were everywhere. "Oh, my God." Caroline's eyes widened as her eyes roamed the lot. There were even news crews.

Jax rode his bike all the way up by the building and parked. Helping Caroline off the bike, he frowned. "Stay close to me," he ordered, his whole personality shifted into Warrior mode. He glanced over at Sid, who had parked next to them. "Mika could be anywhere in this crowd. Make sure everyone stays alert."

"Done." Sid's eyes shifted to the crowd of women who were lining up, waiting to go inside.

Caroline held on to Jax's hand tightly as he ushered her through the crowd to get inside the door. Steve was in charge of letting women inside and opened the door for them.

Jill, Pam, Nicole, and Tessa all stood in different locations interviewing women. Jill's panicked eyes met hers. "It's okay," Caroline mouthed, but in truth, it was pretty damn scary. Impressive, but overwhelmingly scary.

"I want to be Sloan when I grow up." Steve sighed as he opened the door for a beautiful woman who'd just finished being interviewed by Nicole, giving her a sappy grin. "I mean holy hell, will you look at this? Women from everywhere coming to be his secretary."

"Sloan is going to shit bricks when he finds out about this." Sid frowned. "And we'll probably get our asses chewed."

"Why?" Steve looked confused. "What man in his right mind wouldn't love this? Hell, he could have a different secretary every day of the week for a year."

"Do you not know who Sloan is?" Sid glared at Steve. "Have you not been involved in any dealings with the man whatsoever?"

Steve appeared to think about it, nodding. He opened the door for a pretty brunette who patted him on the cheek, giving him a wink. "Well, maybe this is exactly what he needs to loosen the stick up his ass." Steve's eyes stayed on the woman's ass, before they shot wide open. "But please don't tell him I said that. Holy fuck, this is going to get me killed. I can't think straight."

"Steve, shut the hell up," Jax growled, not in the mood for his antics. Caroline, on the other hand, was trying to hide her grin behind her hand.

"Please, Caroline, help us." Jill ran up, handing her a bunch of papers.

"Of course I'll help." She took the papers and a pen. "What do I do?"

"Just ask them these questions and see who you think would qualify. We'll narrow it down from there." Jill glanced out the door. "They're still coming. I'm dead. Sloan is going to kill me."

"Probably." Jax frowned down at her.

"Stop it." Caroline elbowed him in the stomach. "No, he won't. Now, come on. Let's get this done."

"Okay." Jill nodded, but when she turned her back, Caroline looked at Jax with wide "'holy shit'" eyes.

Jax stopped her as she passed him. "Keep aware and if something doesn't seem right, let me know."

"I will," Caroline promised. She went over to a table then nodded toward Steve, who let the next woman inside and pointed her to Caroline's position. "Hi." Caroline had to practically put her head in front of Jax, who had moved close to her, in order to get the woman's attention.

"Hi." The woman smiled at Caroline and then continued to stare at Jax.

"Do you have your resume?" Caroline asked her. She then looked at Jax, who looked very annoyed.

"Oh, yes." The woman handed it to her. "Are you Sloan?" she asked Jax.

"Fuck no, I'm not Sloan," Jax bellowed, his eyes narrowed at the woman.

"Jax!" Caroline scolded, taking the woman's resume.

The woman started to cry. Turning, she then ran out of the warehouse. Steve barely had time to open the door.

"Damn, Jax." Steve frowned over at him. "Take a chill pill, meanie."

"Steve, you want me to smash you through that glass door?" Jax growled. His loud voice dragged everyone's attention to him, then Steve.

"Ah, no." Steve's tone clearly indicated he didn't know whether Jax was serious or kidding, so he wore a terrified smile on his face.

"Then shut the fuck up." Jax crossed his arms after giving Steve that warning, settling against the wall.

Caroline frowned, wondering what was wrong with Jax. She'd seen him rude, but never this bad before. "Why are you being so rude?" she asked'.

Jax just cocked his eyebrow at her without answering.

The next woman came in, handing Caroline her resume. When Caroline attempted to ask her questions, the woman's focus was elsewhere, or rather on every Warrior in the room. Her frustration rising, Caroline observed the woman's gaze flicking to Jax, to Damon, and then to Sid. Jared was on the phone inside on the mats.

"What kind of hours are you available?" Caroline

asked, her voice firm and pen poised, ready to write down her response. When only silence greeted her, she looked up; the woman was still staring at Jared.

"Who is that?"

Caroline frowned, laying down her pen. "Are you here for a job or to gawk at Warriors?" Caroline didn't hold back her attitude. This whole thing was ridiculous.

"I'm here for a job." The woman looked taken aback by being called out.

"Okay, good. I'm asking the questions," Caroline said, then repeated, "What hours are you available?"

"If I'm working for him or any of the Warriors, then I'm available 24/7." The woman gave her a sleazy grin.

Caroline took her resume and tore it in half. "We'll call if interested." She proceeded to wad up the torn resume and tossed it in the trash can, right in front of the woman.

The woman sneered and turned to leave. "Bitch," she said as she walked away.

"Better a bitch than a whore," Caroline hissed under her breath. Hearing Jax chuckle, she threw him a dirty look. "Hush."

"Why are you being rude, Caroline?" Jax mocked her.

The next candidate headed toward her, so Caroline didn't have a chance to say anything back to Jax.

"Hi." Caroline tried to smile, hoping that this wasn't going to be another woman like the last one. "Do you have your resume?"

"Yes, I do." The woman, who was a beautiful redhead dressed in a fresh business suit, handed it to her. "It's a zoo out there."

"It's not much better in here." Caroline snorted, glancing at the woman's professional resume. "Please tell me that you're really here for the job and not a Warrior."

"I'm definitely here for the job," the woman replied. "I've been battling a nasty divorce and I don't need another man, Warrior or not, in my life."

"Thank God." Caroline sighed, but gasped. "I'm sorry. I meant that about you wanting a job, not your divorce."

The woman laughed and stuck out her hand. "I knew what you meant. I'm Becky Spencer."

"I'm Caroline Fitzpatrick." Caroline smiled, shaking her hand. "Wait a minute. Do you have a son who went to Campbell County High, Frankie?"

"Yes." Becky laughed. "I thought you looked familiar."

"How's he doing?" Caroline asked excitedly.

"He's doing okay. He's starting college in the fall." Becky's smile beamed, but then faded slightly. "The divorce hasn't been easy on him, but he's doing okay. I want to thank you for everything you did for him. I know he gave you some problems, but he ended up respecting you. Still talks about you, as a matter of fact. He won't believe I ran into you."

"Well, you make sure to tell him hello for me." Caroline started to ask more, but she heard Nicole's raised voice.

"If you touch my mate one more time, I'm going to throw you out of here on your ass." Nicole growled, blocking Damon from the woman.

Sid and Lana rushed over to defuse the situation.

"I don't want to tell you how to do your business, but you're going about this completely wrong." Becky grimaced at the woman's shrill shrieks as Lana escorted her to the door. "Most of the women out there want to land a Warrior. We all saw Jill on the news when she collapsed on the steps of Town Hall and that Warrior saved her. 90 percent of the women out there want *that* more than the job."

"I'm starting to see that." Caroline frowned, then jumped when the door blasted open, knocking Steve on his ass.

"Jill!" Sloan bellowed, his shirt torn. The rage on his face      made      one      woman      faint.

## Chapter 20

"I take it that's Sloan?" Becky leaned over to whisper to Caroline.

"Yep, that's him." Caroline grimaced when Sloan looked their way.

"Sloan, I can explain." Jill held folders against her chest like a shield.

Slade came in the door, stepping over Steve, who still lay on the floor. He stopped, standing next to Jill.

"No, I don't think you can," Sloan growled, his attention going back to Jill.

"Oh!" One lady fluffed her bleach-blonde hair, walking up to Sloan. "Here's my resume. I'm sure you will find me *well*... qualified."

Jill plucked the resume out of the woman's hand and ushered her toward the door. Steve had finally gotten back up and out of the way. "We'll call you for a second interview if you qualify," Jill whispered, shoving the woman out the door and closing it quickly.

"It got a little out of hand, but we've got it under control now." Jill hurried back to stand in front of

Sloan.

"A little out of hand? Does this look like things are in control?" He pointed to his torn shirt. "I want these women gone and I want them gone now."

"But…" Jill frowned and started to point to the door.

"I said, NOW!" Sloan bellowed, again scaring the woman who had fainted. Tessa was just helping her up, with Jared's assistance.

"Fine." Jill huffed, then grabbed the resumes from the women inside before they left. "We'll call you in a day or two if you qualify for a second interview."

"It was nice seeing you again." Becky smiled at Caroline, glancing at Sloan as she headed toward the door.

"You too, and make sure you tell Frankie I said hello," Caroline called out. Immediately, she bit her lip when Sloan glared at her.

"Uh, I think you've got a problem." Becky hadn't walked outside yet.

Sloan turned and walked to look outside, his size dwarfing Becky. Caroline stood on tiptoe to see what was going on. "Oh, no." In shock, she turned to look at Jax before focusing on the scene unfolding outside. It was a free-for-all as women began fighting each other.

"Son of a bitch." Jax headed toward the door, giving her a stern look. "Do not leave this room."

"Don't worry about that." Caroline raised her eyebrows as the Warriors walked into the biggest catfight she had ever seen.

"Fuck that." Steve stood by the door. "Ain't no way I'm getting in the middle of that crazy shit!"

Jax grabbed him by the neck on his way out the door, tossing him right in the middle of the action.

Caroline, Nicole, Tessa, Pam, Becky, and even Lana, who Sid refused to let help, were the only ones left inside. As one, the women went to the front and watched in shock as the Warriors tried to subdue and calm down over a hundred pissed-off women.

"Is that Angelina?" Nicole pointed against the glass.

"Damn, it is." Tessa was ready to open the door for her. "She had school today and was coming by to help when she was done."

"Adam has her." Nicole sighed in relief. "Get ready to open the door, Tessa. Here they come."

Adam pushed Angelina inside before running back out to help.

"Are you okay?" Caroline steadied Angelina.

"Yeah, but what the hell is going on?" Angelina squeezed herself between the women to watch the mayhem unfold.

"That bitch just smacked Damon." Nicole growled. "Oh, hell no."

Tessa stopped her from going outside. "Nicole, they said to stay inside and that's exactly what we're going to do. They can't do their jobs if they're worried about us."

"But I'm a damn vampire," Nicole hissed. "I'll bite a bitch."

"And that's exactly why they want you inside," Tessa replied. "They're not hurting any of the women. Just separating and calming them down so they don't hurt each other."

Caroline covered a chuckle. This so wasn't funny, but it was. She glanced toward Becky, who was also trying to hide a grin.

"Why's Steve running?" Pam asked.

Caroline turned to find Steve. Indeed, he was running with a look of terror on his face. Behind him, two women were running extremely fast after him, trying to hit him with their purses. Caroline couldn't hold it in anymore. That had to be the funniest thing she'd ever seen. Soon, all the women were laughing, but trying to hide it.

Her eyes met Jax's, who was trying to separate two women who had handfuls of each other's hair. He happened to glance up, his eyes landing on her grinning face, and his eyes narrowed.

She wiped the grin off her face and looked away from him to see Steve had lost the two women and was trying to calm another one down. Obviously, he failed miserably, because she kicked him between the legs and he went down.

"Ohhhh!" the women gasped in unison.

Finally, after what seemed like hours, the Warriors cleared the parking lot without major injury… to the women.

One by one, they walked into the warehouse with torn clothes, scratches on their bodies, and Steve holding his balls.

Caroline and Lana made eye contact and then looked away from each other quickly. She had to bite the inside of her cheek to keep from giggling. Jax stood across the room, glaring at her as if he knew she was trying so hard not to laugh.

"Guess it's safe for me to venture on out." Becky cleared her throat, sounding suspiciously like she was trying not to laugh.

"Jared, make sure she gets to her car," Sloan ordered, glancing briefly at Becky.

"Thank you," she responded, but he only gave a nod.

"I need an ice pack for my boys." Steve broke the silence, still holding his balls with a pained look on his face. "It don't matter, human or vampire, that hurts like a bitch."

That was all it took for the women to burst out laughing, except for Jill, who looked like she was ready to stand in front of a firing squad.

*****

Jax watched Caroline laugh along with the women. He could imagine how it had looked for an observer, but honestly, it was a scary fucking situation. Women were vicious. He'd rather fight two of the biggest bastards than two tiny women.

"I'm going to tell you this one time and one time only." Sloan's tone was low, but the impact was direct. "You will never, and I mean ever, do anything like this again."

"I was just—"

"No." Sloan shook his head, his eyes narrowing dangerously down at Jill. "I don't want to hear anything other than 'yes, sir.'"

Jill crossed her arms, her one foot tapping against the floor. "Can't I just—"

"Dammit to hell, Jill!" Sloan's bellow rattled the walls. "You're suspended indefinitely until you can learn to follow orders."

"Whoa, wait a minute." Nicole stepped up. "I put the ad in the paper. This isn't all her fault."

"It was her idea." Sloan wasn't having any of it.

"Actually, it was all our idea." Tessa and Pam also stepped up beside Jill. Angelina, Lana, and Caroline stepped forward in full support.

"She was only trying to help you," Lana added. "It's not her fault every woman for miles wants a Warrior of their own."

"And I think I've found the perfect person to be your secretary," Caroline added.

"You did?" Jill asked excitedly.

"Which one?" Nicole asked.

"No!" Sloan yelled over them. "Absolutely no!"

"Don't yell at me, Sloan Murphy." Caroline stood up to him. "I'm not one of your Warriors, or a mate."

Sloan glanced at Jax, who just shrugged, cocking an eyebrow as if saying "'you're on your own, bro.'"

"All the other Council leaders have secretaries."

Nicole put a hand on her hip.

"At least interview the woman I think would be perfect." Caroline handed him Becky's resume. "I really don't think you want another catfight. You all didn't fare too well with the last one."

"Can I leave, please?" Steve groaned. "I'm having issues and I sure as hell don't want to get kicked in the balls again. Women fight dirty."

"Damn right we do," Tessa agreed as the rest of the women nodded.

"She really needs work and I know her." Caroline walked up to Sloan. "And Jill doesn't deserve to be suspended. That was a bullshit call, even for you."

Jax grinned, hearing Caroline's words to Sloan. She was right. It was a bullshit call, but he could also see Sloan's point.

"You're bleeding." Caroline walked up to Jax. She reached up, touching a scratch down his cheek. "I'll get a paper towel to clean it."

"Did I see you laughing as you watched out the window?" Jax asked. He tried not to grin at her attempting to cover the fact that she had indeed been laughing at them trying to calm a horde of pissed-off women.

Caroline pulled away from him with false wide-eyed shock. "No, I most certainly wasn't." She sucked at lying. "I was terribly worried for you."

Jax chuckled as he watched her walk away.

"So tell me straight." Jared walked up to Jax. "Did that scare the shit out of you or what?"

"Honestly?" Jax glanced at him. "Yeah, I have to say it did."

"I'd rather—"

"Oh, my God. Caroline!" Lana screamed.

Jax was moving before he even knew what was going on. He was in time to watch Caroline collapse to the floor, her body going stiff as her back curved off the ground. Her eyes were wide open, staring at the ceiling. "Fuck!" Jax slid to the floor on his knees beside her. "Caroline!"

******

Caroline heard someone shouting her name. It was Jax. Her eyes opened, but all she saw was blackness. *Oh, God! This can't be happening again.* Panic set in as she tried to fight her way back to Jax. The blackness was so thick it felt claustrophobic. Suddenly, a hand came out of the darkness.

"Take my hand." Alisha's voice spoke quietly in the blackness.

Caroline started to reach for the hand, but pulled it back. She had been tricked before and it had been terrifying. "How do I know it's really you?"

"Hurry, Caroline." Alisha sounded afraid. "They're coming."

"Who's coming?" Caroline's body began to shake. Even though it felt like a dream, her fear was real. It was real and not a nightmare.

The hand jerked, grabbing her. Caroline screamed in pure terror as she was pulled through the darkness while hands tried to pull her back.

# Chapter 21

"Caroline!" Jax attempted to pick her up, but her body was so stiff he was afraid of hurting her.

"Watch out." Slade knelt beside Caroline, checking her pulse. "Her vitals are stable," he said after checking her over.

Jax looked up at Lana, who cried silently, staring at her sister. "What's happening, Lana?" Jax asked, but when all Lana did was shake her head and cry, his rage broke free. "Goddammit, what in the fuck is wrong with her!?"

A scream of horror escaped from Caroline's mouth as her body was abruptly released from the trance. Her eyes blindly searched for an enemy that wasn't there. Slade and Jax tried to control her flailing arms, but that only made her fight harder and scream louder. She remained in the midst of whatever nightmare she had been in.

"Caroline." Jax tried to get her to look at him, but she fought and fought hard. He was afraid of hurting her.

"Let her go." Slade backed up, letting Caroline fight whatever demon was chasing her. "We're making it worse."

Jax watched helplessly as Caroline battled something he couldn't see, and it about tore him apart, but Slade was right. They were making it worse, trying to subdue her. He watched in anguish as she clambered to her hands and knees. Finally stopping screaming, her breathing was raspy and fast. Clumsily, she pulled herself to the corner of the room with Jax right beside her, but not touching.

"Caroline." He kept his voice low and calm, only inches from her. She huddled in the corner, pulling herself into a ball. "Caroline, it's Jax. Come on, baby, fight it."

Finally, she lifted her head. Her eyes slowly met his. "Jax?" she whispered, her face pale and even though her eyes were clearer, they held a glimmer of terror.

"Yeah, baby." Jax wanted nothing more than to reach out, pull her into the safety of his arms, but reluctantly he held back. He didn't want her to relapse into whatever the fuck that was. Fear for her threatened to consume him. The terror he had felt actually clawed at his throat. He needed her to be okay. He needed the dread shading her eyes to disappear. "It's me." Her hesitation to believe him was like a knife to the gut.

As her eyes became clearer, searching around the room without moving any part of her body, they came back to him. "Jax," she repeated. Her body started to tremble as she reached toward him.

Finally pulling her into his arms, he shielded her body with his as he cocooned his body around hers. "I got you," he whispered against her hair, absorbing her fear as if it were his own.

Jax had no idea how long he sat in the same position holding Caroline, and he didn't care. He would sit there forever if he had to. Her quiet voice broke through the silence, but he couldn't hear the words. "What?" He leaned down closer.

"Where's Lana?" She slowly raised her head to look around.

"Lana," Jax called, still holding Caroline tightly to him.

"Are you okay?" Lana walked over and knelt down.

Jax loosened his grip reluctantly as Caroline sat up. "Alisha."

Lana nodded. "She's here. She pulled you out."

"Pulled her out of what?" Jax asked, not liking the fact he didn't know what the hell was going on.

"Mika has someone like me and Caroline who can see and talk to the dead." Lana frowned. "He's using this woman against us. The dead can take control of people like us when we're vulnerable, and hold us captive in a dream state."

"Like possession?" Jax's eyes widened.

"Not exactly," Lana replied. "I mean, yes, that's possible, but not easy to do and most dead don't do that. But it's easier for them to mess with our subconscious, as I said, and hold us hostage in a dream or trance state."

"How do you fight against that?" Jax growled, his hands fisted at his sides, wanting to pound the threat, but the threat was unseen and it about killed him.

"We can't," Lana answered, glancing down at Caroline. "And you're more vulnerable because it's happened to you before, and not too long ago."

"Are you in danger?" Sid growled to Lana.

"No, I don't think so. He's wanting to control Caroline, which means he can control Jax. Jax is who he really wants," Lana replied, her eyes looking from Sid to Jax.

"The fucker needs to die," Sid hissed, wrapping his arms around Lana.

Jax looked up, meeting Sid's hard gaze before looking back at Lana. "Where's Alisha now?" Jax's eyes narrowed.

"Standing behind you." Lana looked over his head. "Mika promised to let you live if she gave him information, so she started shifting into a little boy to throw Caroline off. She now knows that Mika was lying. She's afraid, Jax, and very confused."

"I don't trust her." Jax was not really sure what he thought about any of this. Never had he believed he would be faced with battling something he couldn't see, yet that was exactly what had happened. He'd been helpless to help Caroline when she needed him most and that was something he couldn't live with.

"She pulled me out, Jax." Caroline broke her silence. "If not for her, I would still be trapped, and honestly, I can't survive going through that again."

"You won't have to." Jax carefully moved her and stood. He faced where Lana had said Alisha stood. "Where's Mika, Alisha? You really want to help me? Tell me where Mika is."

\*\*\*\*\*\*

"Your sister is very strong." The old woman sat in a large chair, staring into nothing.

"My sister is a pain in my ass," Mika spat. "What happened, you old hag?"

"She broke the girl free." The woman's eyes finally met Mika's. "And you best watch how you talk to me."

"Fuck!" Mika stood and paced the room. "I swear I'll kill the little bitch again. Try again. I want Caroline in my control."

"She will just break her free again." The woman snapped her fingers and a cat jumped on her lap. "You need to find another way. I've done what you asked and what you paid me for. I can do no more."

Familiar rage boiled inside Mika and he knew the beast he lived with was just at the surface. "You have no idea who you're dealing with." Mika turned, his black eyes rimmed with red, staring at the woman.

"Oh, but I do," she replied, petting the solid black cat who hissed at Mika. "The dead have plenty to say about you. And don't forget who *you* are dealing with. I may be old but I have much power."

In two strides, Mika was bent over the old woman. Grabbing her by the hair, he pulled her head back. "You will do as I say and you will do it now." Mika snatched her cat, holding it by the throat. A sinister smile bared his sharp fangs. "Do it now or I'll kill your filthy animal before your eyes. I'll then rip your throat wide open. I want Caroline in my control."

******

Caroline stood on shaky legs with Jax's help. She glanced around at everyone, who openly stared at her. "I'm fine." She let go of Jax.

"Are you sure?" Jax watched her closely, making her nervous.

She nodded, then turned toward Lana. "Where is she?"

"After Jax asked where Mika was she disappeared." Lana frowned. "Why don't you go home and get some rest."

"Yeah, I might do that," Caroline replied. Confusion clouded her mind. She looked up at Jax and he looked as if he was fading. Putting her hand to her eyes, she rubbed them and then looked again. It was getting worse. "It's happening again." She grabbed Jax's arms in a tight grip.

"What?" Jax looked at her, surprised. "Don't leave me, Caroline. Fight! Don't you fucking give in!"

While Caroline heard him, it sounded like they were in a tunnel. It was as if she were being pried from him. And she did fight, fought like she had never fought before.

"I can't do this!" Caroline felt her mind slipping into darkness and clawed her way out. She kept her eyes open as long as she could, seeing nothing but Jax yelling for her to fight.

"Fight, Caroline." Alisha's voice overwhelmed her. "You can do this. Fight. You're stronger than you think. Know what's happening and fight it. Go toward Jax."

Caroline came out of it quickly to Jax shaking her. "Jax." She finally opened her eyes. "I'm okay," she lied; she was far from okay.

"Son of a bitch!" Jax pulled her to him, hugging her tight.

Pure anger rushed through her. Pushing away from Jax, she stared into his eyes. "Find your brother and kill that bastard." A moment later, as always happened when she got angry, she cried. She totally lost it as Jax promised to find and kill Mika.

\*\*\*\*\*\*

Mika stepped over the old woman's body. She had failed him, so she'd had to die. That was okay. He'd find another. This wasn't over by a long shot. A hissing noise came from behind him. Turning, he saw the old woman's cat that had escaped from his grip while he had murdered its owner. "Come here, kitty." Mika snapped his fingers, but the cat hissed again before disappearing.

A noise coming from the back of the house had Mika turning quickly. Going to investigate, he heard what sounded like running water. Stopping in the hallway, he looked down to see steam coming from under a door.

With no fear, he kicked it open. The shower had been turned on. The steam-filled room made it hard to see, but as soon as it escaped out of the open door, Mika looked at the mirror.

*Be prepared to die soon, brother.*

*Alisha*

The words were bold, taunting. The rolling condensation down the mirror made the letters look eerily like clear blood drops. "You little bitch!" Mika bellowed. "You think you can threaten me?

Jax is going to suffer and his little bitch is going to die. There isn't a fucking thing you can do about it. I should have made you suffer before I killed you!"

Mika stared at his image in the mirror before punching it, shattering his reflection as well as Alisha's warning.

# Chapter 22

Caroline stood staring in front of her closet. It had been a frustrating four days since she was almost lost to the world again. Her stomach rolled at the thought. Jax had been by her side throughout it all, yet he wasn't present. When she had her in-service days at school, he had driven her, sat outside along with Blaze or whoever else he could find to go with them. He hardly spoke and when he did, it was mumbled responses. He hadn't touched her, barely looked her way. He spent a lot of time on the phone and then he would disappear for small amounts of time, again leaving Blaze or someone else with her.

The only good news came from Lana. Rod had been transferred to the human courts and received five years in prison. It seemed that he had outstanding warrants, which they also tried him for. Jax still hadn't been happy with the results, saying he would be paying Rod a visit the day he was released.

Tomorrow was the first day of school and she needed to find something to wear. Preparation for a new school year was usually an exciting time for her; however, in light of the chaos of recent events, it just seemed dull. Until Mika was taken care of, a life with Jax was doomed. The way Jax was acting toward her the last few days proved that.

"Caroline." Alisha's voice came from behind her.

"Where have you been?" Caroline turned to see

Alisha standing next to her bed. Alisha had disappeared the day at the warehouse and never reappeared, at least to her.

"I've been trying to find out what Mika's up to next, but he's disappeared again." Alisha sounded worried. "I don't know what he's planning, but I'm afraid. He killed that lady."

"What lady?" Caroline frowned, keeping her voice down so Jax didn't hear her talking.

"The one like you." Alisha looked toward the door and then disappeared.

"Who are you talking to?" Jax stood in the doorway.

"Well, I was talking to Alisha, but she left," Caroline replied, drinking in the sight of him.

"Did she say anything about Mika?" His eyes shifted, came back to her then shifted again as if not wanting to look at her too long. Her throat tightened as a sense of doom swept through her body. He had been acting odd and now she knew why.

"No, not really. She said he's vanished, but that's about it." She frowned. If she were a selfish person, she could keep quiet about information, ensuring Jax wouldn't leave, but she wasn't selfish… dammit.

Jax nodded, then turned to leave without saying anything else.

"She also said...," she began and he stopped, turning toward her.

"What?" He crossed his arms, waiting.

"She also said that Mika killed the woman who was like me and Lana. So it seems I'm safe in that aspect." Yeah, there it was. Relief crossed his face as he grabbed his phone, walking away from the door.

"Hey, can you come to Caroline's," she heard him say. "Yeah, I got stuff I need to take care of."

"Is that the only reason you've been sticking around?" Caroline needed to make damn sure she was right about this, but deep in her heart, she knew she was and it was absolutely killing her.

"What?" Jax looked up from his phone, a blank expression on his face.

"For the past four days since that happened to me at the warehouse, you've not touched me, barely talked to me, not to mention look me in the eye for a mere second, and as soon as I tell you the woman who was working with Mika is dead, you're ready to bolt out of here." Caroline laid it all out in the open. She pulled no punches and by damn, she wanted the truth.

His silence said it all. He stared at her, his mouth a firm, straight line across his face.

Anger hit her hard. She walked past him out into the hallway and stomped down the steps. Snatching his jacket and bag, she met him at the bottom of the steps as he came down behind her.

Caroline slammed the bag and jacket against his stomach. "Get the hell out of my house." Thank God her voice held. Inside, she shook so hard, but on the outside she stood firm. He was not going to do this to her again; she couldn't let him do this to her again. Hell, she *refused* to let him do this to her again.

"What's wrong with you?" Jax frowned, grabbing his stuff.

"You are what's wrong with me." Caroline then stomped to the front door and swung it wide open. "I want you out of my house and there better not be any more Warriors showing up here. I can't do this anymore, Jax. If you can't see what you're doing to me, to us, then you need to leave… now."

Jax reached above her head, slamming the door shut. "I am doing my job and I'll leave when I'm damn good and ready."

"I am not your job, Jax." Caroline turned to head toward the kitchen. Opening the drawer, she reached in and then turned, aiming her gun at him. "And I said to get the hell out of my house."

Jax dropped his stuff and walked straight at her until the barrel of the gun jabbed him in the stomach. "Pull the trigger." He tilted his head, a wicked gleam in his eyes. "Do it!" he challenged her in a low voice.

Damn the man. Didn't anything intimidate him, even her aiming a freaking gun at him? Caroline lowered the gun, shaking her head, looking at the floor. "Just leave."

"What do you want from me?" Jax growled.

Her eyes shot up to his. Sadness and loss filled her to such an extreme she almost doubled over, but again, she stood strong. "Something I obviously can't have."

"You're not making any sense." Jax grabbed the gun from her, snorting in disgust because she hadn't even clicked the safety off. Then he chuckled. "No bullets? You're making a habit of pointing this gun at me." He eyed her as he snapped the clip back in place.

"I really didn't want to shoot you. I just wanted you to leave, and I make perfect sense." Caroline turned away from him and grabbed her purse and keys. "As long as Mika is a threat, I can't have what I want and you're too afraid to commit."

"What in the fuck do you think I've been doing for the past month?" Jax threw his hands out to his sides in frustration.

Caroline ignored that; she had to or she'd cave. "What if you never find Mika? What if this goes on for years? Will you hold yourself back from me or anyone who cares for you because of your fear? To me, that's not living life."

"You have no idea what this is really about," Jax hissed, running his hand through his hair.

"No, I don't," Caroline spat out. "Because you won't talk to me."

His phone started ringing as they stood, glaring at each other.

"I love you, Jax," Caroline whispered, but knew he heard her. She so desperately wanted to hear those same words spoken back to her by this man, but knew that wasn't going to happen. Yet, hope was a funny thing. It kept her staring at him, waiting for him to express those same feelings, knowing he wouldn't.

"You knew exactly who I was, how I felt. I never led you to believe anything else." Jax's eyes actually shifted away from hers.

"No, I guess you didn't." That wasn't exactly what she wanted to hear, but she wasn't surprised. This was the real Jax Wheeler and she should never forget that. Caroline headed toward the door, her already broken heart shattering.

"Mika won't give up," Jax hissed at her back.

"Mika has already won." She walked out the door, closing it quietly behind her.

******

Jax stared at the closed door and only moved when he heard her car start. With a curse, he headed outside. "Fuck!" He ran to his bike that she swerved around and barely missed, hopped on, and followed her out of her drive. The more she drove, the more pissed off he became. Not only because she drove like a crazy woman, but for what she'd said in the house.

Did the woman not understand he was focused on keeping her safe? True, he could be an asshole and he'd never claimed he wasn't. Hell, he was asshole enough to piss her off to the point she pulled a gun on him, even though it was unloaded. He actually grinned at that, wondering what would have happened if she really wanted to shoot him. She was an amazing woman; there was no doubt about that.

Blaze appeared, riding beside Jax, having passed them a few seconds after leaving the driveway. Without words, Jax communicated to Blaze, letting him know he was unsure where they were heading. Blaze remained silent, asking no questions, much to Jax's relief.

When Lana had told him Mika's plans to control him through Caroline, Jax had known he needed to find the son of a bitch. Yet he'd felt as if his hands were tied. With Caroline in danger, he'd been unable to leave her long enough to search. But once he'd learned Mika had killed the woman working for him, his need to protect Caroline stepped up a notch. He could finally up his search. Obviously, that hadn't gone over well… at all. He was man enough to admit to himself that her words of love scared the shit out of him. That was such a gift, and he'd pretty much thrown it back in her face, but it had been so long since he had heard those words spoken to him. So long ago he could hardly remember it. Damn, if only he were a man who wasn't terrified of such emotions.

If he were being honest, he was damn proud of Caroline. She'd stood up to him. At first, it had royally pissed him off, but since cooling down, he realized she was protecting herself, just like he was trying to do. The difference was, he was trying to protect her from a lunatic and she was trying to protect herself from him. That knowledge was a punch in the gut.

One thing she was definitely wrong about, or actually two things: He would find Mika, and the fucker hadn't won. He wouldn't win anything but a trip to Hell.

Jax and Blaze slowed as Caroline pulled into the driveway of her parents' house. He pulled over, wanting nothing more than to fix everything, but it wasn't the time. Just as he needed to cool off, so did she. Finally, Caroline exited her car, closed the door, and stared at him as if waiting. When Jax didn't make a move to get off his bike and approach her, she turned and pulled out her cell phone. She focused intently on it, seemingly typing a text as she walked toward the front door. She barely spared a glance at the door before her father opened it.

As soon as she was safely inside, Jax turned to Blaze. "If she leaves, follow her. Keep me updated and if there's any trouble, call me right away."

"No problem." Blaze nodded, then positioned his bike where he could see the house as well as part of the backyard.

Jax nodded his thanks and took one last look toward the house before taking off.

## Chapter 23

Before Caroline could use her key, her dad opened the door. "What a great surprise." He gave her a hug.

"Hey, Dad." Caroline hugged him back. "Where's Mom?"

"In the kitchen. Come on in." He stepped aside and was ready to shut the door, but his cop senses kicked in and he continued to stare toward the driveway. "Is that a friend of yours?"

Caroline looked past her dad to see Jax take off as Blaze stayed, leaning against his bike, his head moving as he scanned the area. "Sort of." Caroline frowned. She really didn't want her dad asking many questions because she didn't want them to worry.

"Sort of?" He narrowed his eyes at her. "He either is or isn't and if he isn't, I need to go find out why he's sitting in front of our house, and if he is, then we need to invite him inside."

Keeping anything from her dad took skill, which was Lana's department, not hers. She could never lie to her dad, which was why when they were younger, Lana left Caroline home while she went out partying. "He's a Warrior, Dad." She tugged him out of the way and closed the door.

"Is there a problem?" He followed her to the kitchen.

"Nope, no problem, Dad." Caroline stepped into the kitchen. "Hey, Mom."

Her mom gave her a hug, then pulled back. "Caroline, you look tired. Have you been sick?"

"No, just been busy with the house and getting ready for school to start tomorrow," Caroline replied with a smile. Her mom missed nothing, just like her dad. "Where's Jamie?"

"Upstairs, trying to find something to wear." Her mom rushed around to finish cleaning up for dinner. "It's her freshman year, so she has to look perfect. You remember those days."

A sadness rushed over Caroline. How simple life had been at that age. Jamie had been what her parents liked to call a "'blessed surprise.'" They had thought after her and Lana they were finished, because, as they liked to tease, "'twins about did them in,'" but life had a different plan for them.

"Will you have her in your class this year?" Her dad sat at the counter, sounding worried that his baby girl was going to high school.

"No, Dad." Caroline laughed. "I teach junior and senior history. Now stop worrying, Jamie's going to be absolutely fine."

"Hey." Jamie came into the kitchen. "There's some dude outside leaning on a bike staring at the house."

"It's a friend of your sister's," her dad replied, still sounding suspicious.

"You ready for school?" Caroline changed the subject.

"I've been ready for high school for a long time." Jamie's voice was high with excitement. "I'm already signed up for cheerleading tryouts. I can't freaking wait!"

Caroline laughed. Indeed, her little sister had been ready, and she blamed herself and Lana for that. Jamie hated being the young one and always tried to be like her and Lana. Caroline had treated Jamie like an older sibling, and Jamie had always been very mature for her age and a little too curious for her own good.

A knock on the door made Caroline jump. Her dad left to answer the door. Between her mom and Jamie, she couldn't hear who it was, so she kept trying to peek down the hallway, secretly hoping it was Jax, but it wasn't.

Blaze followed her father into the kitchen with the phone to his ear. "Yes, sir." His deep voice filled the room as did his body. She happened to glance at her sister and mom, who were giving him the once-over, and she rolled her eyes. What the hell was it with Warriors that had young, middle-aged, old, and married women gaping like they'd never seen a man in their life?

"Honey." Her dad snapped his fingers. "Honey!"

"Yes?" Her mother finally looked his way.

"I'm standing right here," he reminded her, making her blush furiously.

"Well, I know that. My goodness." She snapped a dishcloth at him. "I was just waiting for him to get off the phone to offer him a drink."

Her dad gave a disbelieving snort and winked at Caroline.

"Sloan." Blaze handed her the phone with a cock of his eyebrow. When she just stared at it, he grabbed her hand, put the phone in it, and then raised it to her ear.

"Hello?" She glared at Blaze when she answered. Quickly, she pulled the phone away from her ear with a grimace before putting it back. "You need to stop yelling at me so I can understand you. Yes, I have my phone. It's in my purse. I didn't hear it ring. I don't think it's necessary. Because I don't. That's none of your business. You're yelling again. Fine. Okay. Whatever. Yes." She hung up, then handed the phone back to Blaze.

"Where's your phone?" Blaze didn't attempt to leave.

"In my purse." When he stared at her with no intention of moving or elaborating, she sighed, turned, and dug into her purse to find it. Finding it, she held it up toward Blaze, wiggling it as if saying 'there, ya happy?' "Why did you tell Sloan you knew where I was? You got me yelled at."

"I don't lie to my superior." Blaze frowned down at her. "And did you or did you not text him, which he was calling to follow up with you about?"

Caroline wanted so badly to stick her tongue out at Blaze, but swallowed her desire. She had texted Sloan as soon as she got to her parents' house to tell him to keep Jill, Steve, and Adam out of her classroom. She was fine and didn't need them there. Obviously, he wasn't happy with simply texting her back so he'd tracked her down.

"I'm Miles Fitzpatrick." Her dad stuck his hand out to Blaze. "This is my wife, Melanie, and daughter, Jamie."

"Blaze," was his one-word response, but he did shake her father's hand and nod to her mom and sister.

Caroline glanced at her sister, who was biting her fist, then looked at her and mouthed, "'Oh, my God'" after Blaze turned back to their dad. Her mom actually gave her a wide-eyed look and a nod as if asking if she and Blaze were an item, which Caroline shook her head to with narrowed eyes.

"So, Blaze"—her father crossed his arms across his chest—"can I ask who you are and why you are standing guard outside my house? Is my daughter in some kind of danger I need to know of?"

"You a cop?" Blaze's voice was even, his eyes never leaving her dad's.

"Actually, I'm a dad to three girls, but yes, I am a cop." Her father eyed Blaze, not intimidated in the least.

"Retired cop," her mom piped in.

A smile spread across Blaze's handsome face and Caroline was worried her mom and sister were going to faint. "I was ordered to—"

"Rod has been coming around again," Caroline answered with a half lie. "Sid wanted to make sure that one of the Warriors kept an eye on me."

"You need to get a restraining order against him." Her mother frowned.

"It's okay, Mom," Caroline replied, grabbing her purse. "It's taken care of now. I need to get going, got a busy day tomorrow. I just wanted to stop by to see if Jamie wanted a ride to school with me."

"Jamie," her mom said, but Jamie was staring at Blaze. "Jamie Lynn, your sister is talking to you." Her mother nudged her, then smiled at Blaze.

"What?" Jamie seemed to snap out of it.

"Do you want a ride to school tomorrow?" Caroline couldn't help but grin. She totally knew what her sister was going through. She found herself doing the same thing with Jax. She frowned at the thought.

"No, I'm riding with Mary and her sister." Jamie's gaze went back to Blaze.

"Okay, well if you need anything, just head up to my classroom." Caroline hugged and kissed her mom, Jamie, and then turned toward her dad, who was staring at her with the "'I know you're lying'" father look.

"I'll walk you to the door." Her dad held out his hand for her to go ahead.

Once they were on the porch, her dad closed the door behind him. "I don't know what the hell is going on, but I know you're lying because Rod has been sentenced to prison. Yeah, I still have my connections and keep track of things." He stared at her for a long minute before pulling her into his arms. "But I know your sister and Sid, as well as this young man, will make sure you're taken care of. Whenever you're ready to talk, I'm here and if you need help, you yell and I'm there."

"Thanks, Dad." Caroline hugged him tight. "It's really fine. Just a precaution."

"Take care of my girl," Miles ordered Blaze.

"Yes, sir." Blaze once again shook her father's hand.

Caroline had never been so happy to be inside her car and driving home. That had been a complete disaster. She had wanted to go to her parents' house for a minute of peace, to have a minute of normal, but that sure as hell didn't happen.

Before long she was back home with Blaze following her down the driveway. She climbed out of the car and headed to the house, but Blaze stopped her.

"Let me go in first." He opened the door, did a once-over, and focused as he looked around once again. She walked in behind him and stopped when he held up his hand. He went upstairs and was back in a second flat. "It's clear."

Caroline watched him head toward the door. "Where you going?"

"Outside." He nodded, passing her.

"Why?" she asked, confused. "You don't have to stay outside."

"Bro code." Blaze grabbed the door as he started to pull it shut.

"Bro code?" She frowned. "You're very handsome, Blaze, but I don't plan on seducing you."

"You belong to Jax," Blaze said bluntly. "I stay outside." He closed the door behind him.

Tears slowly filled her eyes. How she wished that were true. Caroline went into the kitchen, flipped on the radio, and then headed for the couch, grabbing her purse on the way. She dug for her phone, checking to see if she had any messages. Nothing, and the only recent missed calls were from Sloan. Tossing the phone next to her, she snorted. What had she expected, a call from Jax, maybe a text? He had barely talked to her, then she'd thrown him out of her house at gunpoint no less. She'd be lucky if she ever saw him again.

Mentally exhausted, Caroline lay down on the couch, thoughts nagging at her. Had she really been fair to Jax? Had she been too needy? Should she have just sucked it up and taken what he offered, no matter her feelings? Could she love enough for both of them? Those thoughts, mixed with her tears, lured her into a fitful sleep.

## Chapter 24

Returning to Caroline's over an hour previously, Jax had sent Blaze back to the compound. Watching her sleep, his fingers itched to touch her, but he fought it. She was absolutely beautiful. She needed her sleep and he honestly didn't know if she would welcome his touch.

He, along with Sid and Duncan, had searched; he had even shifted, trying to hit the local shifter hangouts to get any leads they could, but Mika had once again disappeared, just as Alisha had told Caroline.

This situation was dire because he had absolutely no idea how to find his brother. Shifters were a special breed. If they didn't want to be found, you wouldn't find them. He'd done the same years ago.

Mika could have been standing right in front of him as a different person and he never would have known it. Damn, he sure could use Hunter right now. As a wolf shifter, he was the best at hunting bastards down, whether they shifted or not; that was what Hunter was trained to do.

Leaning his head back, he closed his eyes. He wanted this done. He wanted Caroline safe. He *wanted* to kill his bastard of a brother.

"What are you doing here?" Caroline's voice was soft from sleep and confused. "I thought I kicked you out."

Slowly, he leaned forward and opened his eyes to see her still resting in the same position, but her eyes were open. "You did," he replied. Unmoving, he sat and stared at her. "I don't follow orders very well."

Caroline closed her eyes as if going back to sleep. A sweet, exhausted sigh escaped from her lips as she pushed herself up into a sitting position. "Jax, I haven't changed the way I feel."

"As you shouldn't," Jax replied, moving to lean forward, putting his arms on his knees. "I'm a son of a bitch, but I'm also good at what I do and have to have room to do it."

"I'm not asking for your soul." Caroline rubbed her eyes before looking at him.

"Too late," Jax whispered, "because you already have it."

Caroline's hands dropped from her face to stare at him. "I don't understand you, Jax." Her bottom lip trembled.

"I've heard that my whole life." It was true. No one had ever understood him. "I'm not an easy man. That's why I stay away from any type of commitment other than my oath to the VC Warriors."

"Then why are you here?" A tear slipped down her

cheek. "Why do you keep coming back? Why do you keep doing this to me?"

"Because I'm a selfish bastard," he replied honestly, reaching out to swipe the tear from her soft skin. "I could sit here and tell you that I can change, that I will be the man you want me to be, but I can't do that. This is who I am, Caroline."

"I don't want you to change the man you are, Jax." Caroline shied away from his touch. "Until your brother is caught, there's no way we can even see if anything can happen between us. I can't sit here and wait to see if you are going to disappear. I can't keep handing you my heart only to have it shoved back at me. I can feel when you pull away. I know when you're becoming distant, and I know it's only a matter of time before you walk out the door."

He watched her stand, having no words.

"As you can't change the man you are, I can't change the woman I am." Caroline's voice cracked. "I want more from you. Guess I'm also a selfish bastard." She smiled sadly as she threw those words back at him, her tears falling.

Jax remained seated, staring at the empty spot on the couch where Caroline had been. Even though his eyes hadn't moved, he knew exactly where Caroline was in the house and what she was doing, but not because he could read her. He had tried. Lana had taught her the art of blocking well. No, he knew exactly where and what she was doing when he was near her because that was how in tune he was to her. He dropped his head to stare at the floor between his booted feet and for the first time in his life, he was at a total loss of what to do.

\*\*\*\*\*\*

Caroline walked into her classroom and set her things down. She hadn't been able to do a lot to organize herself because of how busy she had been, but she wasn't worried. She had made all the in-service days, but fell short getting her classroom ready. Heading to the window to look out at the parking lot, she found Jax talking to Jill, Adam, and Steve. Students had started pulling in and what she usually found exciting about the first day of school, felt dull.

She hadn't been able to sleep after she and Jax had talked, if you could even call it talking. She was still just as confused. She had stayed up in her room until it was time to get ready and leave. Jax had not been in the house, but when she closed and locked the door behind her, she'd seen him on his bike watching her. The whole drive to school felt awkward as he followed, so when she got out of her car in the parking lot, she told him good-bye and to have a nice day, feeling like an idiot the whole time, but dammit, she didn't know what else to do. In a space of twenty-four hours, she'd told him to leave, held a gun on him, explained that she didn't need the Warriors' help, and had even been screamed at by Sloan.

As Jill, Adam, and Steve moved away from Jax, he continued to sit on his bike, his eyes searching the parking lot. With a snap of his head, he looked straight to her window, his intense gaze pinning her to the spot. She was the first to look away. The warning bell buzzed, making her jump. She turned to see a few kids had already made their way into the room.

"Sit wherever you want." She smiled at the students as she headed toward her desk.

"Hey, Ms. Fitzpatrick!"

"Good morning, Jason." Caroline smiled. "How was your summer?"

"Too short." He grinned, taking a seat in the back.

"Yeah, I know what you mean." She laughed. "Come on, everyone, find a seat."

Jill, Adam, and Steve walked in, with Steve giving her the thumbs up. "Hey, teach." He gave her a knowing grin.

Caroline shook her head, then smiled at Jill.

"Hey, I know you." Jason pointed at Adam. "You're Adam Pride. Didn't you already graduate?"

Caroline and Jill made eye contact while Steve looked suddenly nervous.

"Actually, I know all three of you." Jason looked at Caroline. "They're VC Warriors. I saw them on the news."

The classroom erupted into loud conversation as Jill, Adam and Steve found seats, all eyes on them.

"Class!" Caroline tried to regain control. "Quiet!"

Once everyone settled, Caroline continued. "Adam, along with Jill and Steve, do belong to the VC Warriors. They're here to catch up on some of their credits," she lied, hoping it was convincing because she couldn't think of anything else.

"Well, damn, man, that sucks," Jason said, while a few others agreed. "I wouldn't think you'd need any more school, being badass Warriors."

"Everyone needs an education, Jason," Caroline added. "And watch your language in my class." She then grabbed her attendance book and started taking roll call.

As the day wore on, Jill, Adam, and Steve didn't leave her classroom unless she left, then one would go with her. Each and every new class knew who they were because of seeing them on television. The same questions were asked throughout the day. It was very distracting. At lunch, they stuck to her like glue, drawing curious glances from students and teachers.

Toward the end of the day, she was exhausted and

also very unnerved as she looked into the faces of each of her students. Having Jill, Adam, and Steve shadowing her every move put into perspective that maybe she had been wrong in thinking Jax was overreacting about his brother. It was different seeing the faces of her students who were innocent in all of it.

Her life had definitely taken a different turn and it had taken seeing her students to make her realize that. She loved to teach, but it was wrong for her to do so and put her kids, as well as the staff, in danger. If Jax and Sloan felt it was important enough to plant three Warriors, then she needed to be responsible enough to know when she needed to step away for the safety of others.

The last bell of the day rang. Her heart was heavy as she watched each student leave, some saying good-bye while others hurried out the door. Her eyes met Jill's, then Steve's and Adam's, who sat staring at her.

"Well, let me be the first to say that sucked ant balls. I sure am glad I'm just pretending to learn something, because no offense, teach, history is boring as hell." Steve stretched, standing up. When Adam gave him a look, Steve held up his phone. "Yes, ants have balls. I checked, remember?"

"Are you okay, Caroline?" Jill asked, standing and walking toward her.

One of the janitors walked in, emptying her cans

before walking back out. Caroline watched him with a frown. Usually Pete talked to her, but maybe he felt she was busy, with Jill, Adam, and Steve still being there.

"Yeah, I'm fine," she lied. "I need to go to the office for a few minutes. Can you guys meet me outside, please?"

Jill looked toward Adam, then back to Caroline. "I don't know," she replied with a frown. "One of us is supposed to be with you at all times."

"I'll be fine." Caroline grabbed her stuff. "Please."

Adam stood and walked toward her. Reaching out, he touched her arm. "We'll wait for you outside the door."

Caroline nodded. "Thank you."

Adam nodded and headed out the door with everyone following them. He turned, running into the janitor.

"Hey, my bad." Adam reached out, steadying him.

"Pete, are you okay?" Caroline also helped steady the older janitor.

"I'm fine, ma'am." He nodded, then headed quickly down the hall, pushing his cart.

"Damn, Adam." Steve messed with Adam. "Knock the poor old man down, you big bully."

"Shut up, Steve." Adam smacked him upside the head. They all headed to the office and true to his word, Adam made Jill and Steve head outside with him.

"Hey, Caroline." Brenda, Principal Sparks's secretary, gave her a tired smile as she made her way into the office. "How was your first day?"

"It was fine, Brenda," Caroline replied, shutting the door behind her. "Is Matthew in his office?"

"Not yet." Brenda motioned her toward his office. "He'll be back as soon as the buses load. Go ahead and go in. He should be back any minute."

"Hey!" Jamie strolled in to the office. "Can I ride home with you today? My ride had to do something and I really don't want to ride the bus."

"Sure," Caroline replied. "I just have to talk to the principal first. Wait for me at the car. I'll be there in a minute." Caroline tossed her the keys.

"Okay, can we stop and get something to eat?" Jamie caught the keys. "I'm freaking starved. Mom and Dad are going out tonight so I'm on my own."

Caroline nodded at her sister, noticing Pete again who was also staring at Jamie. "Hello, Pete." She smiled as she passed him. "You sure you're okay?"

"Oh, I'm fine, ma'am." Pete grabbed another can before heading back out without even looking at her.

Caroline frowned, watching him disappear out of the office. Brenda shrugged and shook her head when Caroline looked in her direction. Walking into the principal's office, she sat down, her mind going a mile a minute, wondering how one quit a job they loved more than anything.

\*\*\*\*\*\*

"You better hope Jax doesn't find out we let her out of our sight," Jill mumbled to Adam as they stood outside, waiting for Caroline on the steps.

"Yeah, I like my ass just the way it is and if we screw this up, none of us will have an ass left, because once Jax gets done with us, Sloan will...." Steve frowned, pacing around.

"Will you both shut the fuck up?" Adam growled. "I'm reading her right now. If anything happens, I'll know it."

"Ha! You are a fucking genius!" Steve pointed at Adam.

A passing teacher heard Steve's words. "In the office, young man."

"What?" Steve dropped his arm, looking confused.

"We don't use language like that." She ushered him toward the doors.

"Hey, yo!" Steve looked back at Jill and Adam. "A little help here."

"We don't even know you." Jill shrugged, a gleam in her eye.

"I think some time in detention will do you some good." The teacher ignored Steve.

"Ah, shit. Are you serious?" Steve glared at her.

"You just added two more days." She opened the door, pulling him inside.

Jill laughed when she heard Steve say "dammit" before the door closed. Then she looked to Adam, who was focused but grinning.

"Anything?" she asked as she scanned the area.

"No, she's just waiting for the principal," Adam replied, his grin gone as he closed his eyes to focus.

"Wish she'd hurry up." Jill sat down with a huff. "Steve was right. This did suck ant balls. I always hated school."

## Chapter 25

Jax pulled into the school parking lot next to Caroline's car. School had obviously ended, but there was no sign of Caroline. He glanced over to see Adam's car.

His attention turned to a girl walking across the parking lot, but slowing the closer she got to Caroline's car, eyeing him. Instead of going to the driver' side where he sat on his bike, she went to the passenger side and unlocked the door. *Smart girl.*

She looked over the hood of the car at him as she tossed her stuff in the seat. "You waiting for my sister?"

"I am." He nodded. "You must be Jamie."

"I am." She nodded back.

Jax couldn't help it, he laughed. Not only did she look like her sisters, but the attitude matched as well. "I'm Jax. Nice to meet you."

"You a Warrior?" She squinted in the sun as she looked him up and down over the car.

"Yes," he replied, his eyes leaving hers to the car pulling up to them.

"Hey, Jamie!" a boy much older than Jamie slowed

with his arm hanging out the window, trying to appear cool. "You need a ride home?"

"No, she's got a ride." Jax frowned at the kid, then bared his fangs, leaning forward.

The kid drove off, squealing tires with a "'just shit his pants'" look on his face.

"Hey, I might have wanted a ride from him." Jamie walked around the car with her arms crossed in front of her.

"He was too old for you and you know it." Jax narrowed his eyes at her, but a small grin tipped his lips. Yeah, she was just like her sisters, that was for damn sure.

"So answer me this, Warrior." She leaned a hip against the car. "With the Warrior at my parents' house last night, three of them in her classroom today, and you waiting by the car, how much trouble is my sister in?"

****** 

"What can I do for you, Caroline?" Matthew Sparks came into the office, a friendly smile at seeing her. "I hope your first day of school went well."

"It went very well, thank you," Caroline replied, but a return smile just wasn't happening.

He took a seat behind his desk and leaned back in his chair, watching her closely. "The look on your face says different."

"There are some things going on right now that I'm afraid are going to interfere with my job." The words stuck in her throat. "I'm going to have to resign effective immediately."

Matthew rubbed his chin thoughtfully. "Caroline, if I thought the students were in any danger, I never would have allowed Sloan to plant three Warriors in your classroom."

Surprised by his loose use of Sloan's name, Caroline frowned. "You know Sloan Murphy?"

"Very well, actually." Matthew smiled. "Intimidating man, but I have much respect for him. Ever since the integration of vampires into the public school system, I've been working closely with him as well as other Council members. I am lobbying to have at least one Warrior in the school at all times, but Sloan said they're spread too thin to release any Warrior here full time. Though he found a security guard, a vampire, who will be here in case of any problems."

"Oh." Caroline realized she was a little clueless to how everything within the Warrior world worked.

"He called me asking my opinion on your job, about planting Warriors in your classroom as a precaution after explaining to me the situation," Matthew continued. "I trust Sloan as well as his Warrior's and had no problem. He felt the danger to the students was nonexistent, but the danger to you warranted protection. This is a new world we live in, Caroline. I feel safer with Warriors in my school, actually."

Caroline sat absorbing everything she was being told. She felt somewhat better, but still that nagging fear that something could happen to one of her students wouldn't leave her.

"This is your choice, Caroline." Matthew sat forward, his voice sincere. "If you are uncomfortable, I have a sub who can fill in immediately; actually, she's driving me crazy wanting something. But know your job will be waiting for you and I will refuse your resignation. We'll just call it a leave of absence."

"Thank you." Caroline's voice hitched and her eyes burned with tears. "I just can't take the chance of someone getting hurt because of my stubbornness."

"And I respect you more for that." Matthew looked through his Rolodex, pulled out a card. "Consider it taken care of, though I will say I'm just a little disappointed. It was nice having Adam Pride back in Campbell County. I was hoping maybe he could play in some of the football games." He chuckled.

"I don't think that would be fair for the other team." She smiled at the thought. She had never had Adam in any of her classes and wasn't a big football person, but she had heard his name being announced over the intercom during Adam's football days.

"Maybe not, but one can hope." Matthew grinned with a wink. "That state championship trophy would for sure find a new spot in our trophy case out front."

"And that would be cheating," Caroline reminded him as she stood, her legs shaking with relief. She wasn't losing her job and for that, she was grateful.

"Yeah, well, it's your fault I won't be able to try," Matthew teased, standing up with her, and then walking her toward the door.

Caroline stopped at the closed door and turned. "Thank you again." Caroline felt her eyes water with tears. "I really didn't want to leave my job. I love teaching here."

"I wasn't going to let you resign anyway." Matthew opened the door for her. "'Your job is here for as long as it takes."

She nodded, hoping it wouldn't be long at all. She was disappointed to miss even a single day, but it had to be this way. She walked out into the office to see Steve standing with a teacher and secretary, who was writing something down.

"Steve?" Caroline frowned. "What did you do?"

"Nothing." Steve held his hand up in the air. "I did absolutely nothing."

"He was using foul language," the teacher replied with a disapproving frown.

Caroline looked toward Matthew, who just shook his head with a smile. "Go on, I'll take care of this."

"Come on, Steve." Caroline headed for the door, trying not to laugh. Once outside, her laugh burst free. "How in the world can you get detention on the first day of school?"

"All I said was…" Steve saw another teacher coming out of the school and clamped his mouth shut.

"If you could keep your mouth closed for a second, you wouldn't find yourself in trouble all the time." Jill rolled her eyes as they made their way down the steps and out to the parking lot.

Adam was quiet, but kept looking at Caroline.

Caroline saw Jax talking to her sister and her heart skipped a few beats. How the sight of him affected her still surprised her. Just the sight of him sent her emotions into overdrive.

"You ready?" she asked her sister, her eyes leaving Jax's as she gave him a nod.

"Why were you in Principal Sparks's office?" Jamie asked, not moving.

"I, ah…." Caroline frowned, wondering why she was answering to Jamie, who was acting like their mother—or rather, like their father. "I had business to take care of."

"She tried to quit her job," Adam blurted out.

"You what?" Jamie's eyes grew wide. "What the heck, Caroline. What happened? You love this job. Mom is going to freak and Dad is going to have a cow."

"What happened?" Jax repeated one of Jamie's questions. When Caroline didn't answer, he looked to Adam. "What happened?" he repeated.

"She's afraid for her students and the staff," Adam replied, giving Jax a rundown of her conversation.

"You were outside. How do you know this?" Caroline asked, confused and a little pissed off. Then it hit her. "Were you reading me? But I was blocking. I'm always blocking."

"It was the only way I could let you be out of sight, so yes, I read you," Adam answered, without looking a bit sorry. "And if I've had contact with you, which I did right before we left the room, then I can read you even if you block or someone blocks you."

"Well, stop it." Caroline pointed at him. "You're not allowed to do that to me anymore, Adam Pride. And I didn't quit. I'm just taking a little leave of absence."

"If it's my orders, I can't promise anything." Adam shrugged as if he didn't care, but the tone of his voice said he meant every single word he'd just spoken.

"Did you give him orders to do that?" Caroline then pointed at Jax.

"Actually, I'm innocent in this, although… he did exactly what he was supposed to do. They all three had specific orders not to let you leave their sight." He glanced at all three of them. "So even though they broke orders by letting you out of their sight—"

"It was his idea." Steve made sure Jax knew exactly who was at fault. "Totally his call on that one."

"Adam found a way to watch you without being in the same room," Jax finished, ignoring Steve. He glanced at Adam. "Good job, Adam."

"What I want to know is when I'm going to get a supercool power so I can get a 'Good job, Steve'?" Steve huffed, crossing his arms over his chest in irritation.

"You can't do anything?" Jamie asked, looking up at Steve.

"No, not yet, other than get in trouble… which is a lot and something I do very well," Steve mumbled. "I'm pretty much an expert at that."

"Let's go, Jamie." Caroline walked around Jax, who

got off his bike. "I thought you were starving."

"Adam, take my bike," Jax ordered, taking the keys out of Jamie's hands before she could give them to Caroline. "Jill, Steve, take Jamie." He reached in the car to grab her stuff and then handed it to her.

"Why does Adam get to take your bike?" Steve snorted. "I never get to do the cool shit."

"You want to die?" Jax glared at him.

"Not particularly." Steve took two steps back, looking wary. "Wait a minute. Is this a trick question?"

"Be happy you're not doing the cool thing by taking my bike, because if Adam puts one scratch on it, he dies." Jax took Caroline by the arm, leading her to the passenger side of the car.

"Oh, ho!" Steve pointed at Adam. "See you on the other side, biotch."

Adam rolled his eyes as he got on Jax's bike. "Where do you want me to take it?"

"Drop it at Caroline's." Jax had opened the door, but Caroline glared at him, not getting in. "Jill and Steve can pick you up. You guys take Jamie to get some food and then take her home."

"Are you finished?" Caroline waited until he'd

stopped giving orders. "Because this wasn't my plan."

"It is now." Jax used his body to edge her to the car to the point she had to sit down or fall into the vehicle.

Caroline was too tired and stressed to fight. Plus, she knew she would lose and she was just a little curious about Jax's actions.

He got in, adjusted the seat back, and then started her car. He glanced over, his eyes traveling down her body before returning to her face. And oh, how that look burned her, making her forget she was trying to forget him. Hell, who was she kidding? The man was burned into her memory forever and no matter what, it would remain.

"Seat belt," he said, but his eyes said something entirely different as they roamed over her again.

"Stop looking at me like that." Caroline huffed as she put her seat belt on.

"I've never met anyone like you." Jax continued to stare at her.

His words came out of the blue and made her stomach flutter with pleasure. If she wasn't careful, she'd be on his lap before they left the school parking lot. What was she thinking? She couldn't be on his lap, period. She'd made her decision, hadn't she? Dammit, she had to control this situation.

"What? No other woman has ever kicked you out of her house?" she replied with raised eyebrows.

"No, you're the first to have done that, but that's not what I mean." Jax grinned, putting the car in drive, but didn't move. "You know the danger and decided to leave a job you love in order to keep people you care about safe."

"Yes, that's exactly..." Caroline gasped, her stomach pitched and she felt like she was going to be physically ill. "What you have been doing."

## Chapter 26

Jax sat at Caroline's kitchen table waiting for her. She had been upstairs for half an hour, but he was giving her time. Finally, he heard her coming down the stairs.

She walked straight to the table and sat before him. "I owe you an apology."

"No, you don't," Jax replied, placing his phone on the table between them. "Just know that I mean you no harm. I don't want to hurt you in any way."

"I know that, Jax." Caroline sighed. "I think I understand how you feel. I love my students, even the pain-in-the-ass ones who drive me nuts, and I would do anything to help or keep them safe. So I understand why you want to distance yourself from people because of your brother."

"But you've been right," Jax admitted, leaning back in the chair. "I do give my brother too much power. I'm here to protect you and I need to stop letting him dictate my life."

"What happened between the two of you and Alisha?" Caroline's voice was hesitant, yet her eyes begged for the answer.

"I don't talk about my past or my tribe too much because we believe it's disrespectful to the dead." Jax frowned.

"And I respect that, Jax." Caroline nodded. "Even though the history teacher in me as well as someone who cares about you wants to know all about you, I do understand some of the traditions."

"My brother was evil, even when young. The things I've seen him do I would never discuss with you." Jax's anger bubbled at the surface, rising to the level it had been over a hundred years ago. "I had him kicked out of the tribe. He ended up with another tribe and came back for his revenge." The pain in his voice was thick.

"Jax, you don't need to tell me this." Caroline stopped him. "I'm sorry I even asked."

Jax didn't want to tell her. He wanted to forget, but the urge to tell her was strong. He hadn't spoken about this to anyone, ever. Only his sister knew. "I was out hunting when he came back with renegades. They killed everyone in camp. From the very young to the very old. Only a few escaped. Alisha was one of the few."

"I'm so sorry." She reached out, touching his arm.

"I searched for him, hunted him, but it wasn't until Alisha and I were being initiated into the VC Warriors that I finally found him." Jax lifted his gaze to hers and saw his own pain reflected in her eyes. "He killed Alisha before I even knew he was there, going through the initiation with us. He never even tried to kill me."

Jax knew she could hear, actually feel his hatred, but she remained quiet.

"Before I could kill him, the other Warriors stepped in," Jax hissed. "I was so close to my revenge as my sister lay dead at my feet. He had taken everyone away from me, as I had done to him. His last words to me were, 'I will take everyone from you for as long as you walk this earth.'"

\*\*\*\*\*\*

As Caroline listened, her heart broke for him. Yet anger so fierce burned her soul. "And that's what you live with every day." It wasn't a question, but a cold, clear fact.

"Yes," Jax said bluntly.

She didn't know what to say. What could she say? He'd lost his family, friends, and then his sister to a brother who wanted to make him pay for the rest of his life by taking those he cared for away from him. Until that moment, she hadn't fully understood why Jax was reluctant to have a relationship with anyone, even after realizing she had done the same thing in a way. But understanding hit her hard, anger and sadness for the man who sat in front of her rushing through her.

Standing, she wrapped her arms around his neck and pulled his head against her stomach, holding him tight. "I hope you find him and take back your life, Jax Wheeler. No one deserves to live this way." She paused, finding the courage to continue. "If you need to leave"—Caroline held him tighter as if by saying the words he would disappear—"I understand. I'm willing to take the risks just to be with you, but I will understand and will be here waiting for you when—"

Jax didn't let her finish. He pulled her down on his lap, his mouth crashing down on hers. She welcomed him as he was with no other questions asked.

"The risks are too great, but I can't stay away from you." He lifted his mouth long enough to say those words. "I couldn't protect my tribe or my sister so I know this is a big mistake."

"You're more prepared now than you were then. You're a Warrior who's stronger and smarter than Mika. *You* know this and *I* know this. I have faith that you can keep me safe, but it'll be hard always looking over our shoulders." Caroline kissed his chin. "You need to focus on finding Mika. I'm sorry I didn't understand before, but I do now."

"That was my fault." Jax looked into her eyes. "I should have told you from the start, but—"

Caroline interrupted him with a kiss. "Thank you for trusting me enough to tell me."

Jax's eyes shifted from her. "I know you think I don't have feelings for you, but you're wrong."

Caroline pulled his gaze back to her. "I know now, Jax."

"I won't let anything happen to you." His tone became hard, the truth of his words in his eyes.

"I know that also. Actually, I've always known that." Caroline focused on the outline of his tattoos under his white T-shirt. She traced it with her finger, then lifted it to pull it off so she could study them further. Thankfully, he didn't stop her. She had wanted to ask him about them so many times, but Jax without a shirt turned her brain to mush. "What do your tattoos mean?"

Jax swallowed hard. "They're my tribe's symbol with the name of each person that my brother killed worked into it."

He allowed Caroline to pull his shirt over his head. Once more, she traced each tattoo that she could reach. She found Alisha's name beautifully blended into the tribal tattoo over his heart. A tear slowly escaped from her eye.

"It's beautiful." She looked up at him. "A beautiful tribute."

Caroline touched his face, moving his hair back. Her fingers caressed each line and tiny scars as if memorizing every detail.

"Make love to me, Jax," she whispered.

Jax picked her up, collected his phone without looking, and carried her up the staircase. He gently laid her on the bed. Removing his gun, he placed it on the table next to the bed. They undressed each other slowly, exploring and taking time enjoying each other.

His hands were magic against her skin and she felt special. He made her feel beautiful, even with her not-so-perfect body. The way he touched her, his hands trailing over her skin, filled her with excited anticipation. Jax was a quiet man by nature, but his whispered words when he touched her made her feel as if she were perfect. In the past, she had felt self-conscious, as if she didn't measure up to other women, but not with Jax.

She pulled him close, holding him tightly against her. She loved the feel of his hardness against her softness. It made her feel safe. Kissing his way down her body, she cherished the contact.

"I love your body," he whispered against her mouth when he came back for a kiss. "It was made for me."

"You make me feel beautiful." She moaned when his fingers found her sweet spot.

"You are beautiful. It has nothing to do with me." Jax growled, nipping her shoulder with his fangs.

"Why have you never taken my blood?" Caroline asked curiously.

Jax's darkened eyes glowed in response to her question. "Wasn't sure if you wanted that."

"I think I offered it before, and you are a vampire." Caroline raised an eyebrow. "No pressure, I was just wondering."

Jax moved between her legs. "You honor me," he said, right before he rammed inside her at the same time he bit into her neck.

A short scream escaped her throat, but soon turned into needy moans. His aggressive pulls at her neck as he kept a steady, hard rhythm inside her, pushed her closer to the edge.

His fangs left her skin, leaving her gasping and writhing beneath him. After licking her neck, he threw his head back as he rode her hard. When he looked back down at her, the intensity in his eyes had Caroline meeting his thrusts with a strength and power she didn't know she had.

Jax reached under her, grasping her ass to help her slam against him. She knew by the look on his handsome face that he was on the edge, as was she. Holding back, she waited. Gazes locking, it was time. She let herself go, giving herself to him with no regret.

Reaching up, she cupped his face with her hands. "I can love enough for both of us if you let me."

And she knew it was true. She had been fooling

herself. She loved Jax more than anything and whatever it took, she was going to do, because she was afraid that living without him would be like living without air.

"*Ktuhwhunoohmuh,*" Jax whispered into her hair.

"Oh, that's beautiful." Caroline's eyes widened. "What does it mean?"

"It means I love you." Jax rose up to look into her eyes. "I think I've loved you since the day you pounded on my door at the compound, demanding I teach you how to play the guitar."

Caroline's hands flew to her face as uncontrollable sobs took control over her body. They were words she had longed for but never thought she'd hear, but then something he said floated through her muddled mind. Her hands left her tear swollen eyes so she could look at him. "You think?"

"Yeah, for someone who doesn't really know what the hell love is, it took me longer than most to figure it out." Jax gave her a sad smile, then held her close. "I'm sorry for hurting you."

Finally getting herself under control, she wrapped her arms around him. "I've hurt you too, Jax. I'm also sorry." She sniffed, trying not to lose it again. "Do over?" she asked, hopeful.

Jax thought for a minute as a grin spread across his face. "If a do over means when you, how did you say it, sucked my—"

Caroline smacked him on the arm but grinned in amusement. "Yes, even that."

Jax winked at her. "Then definitely yes, a do over."

"And speaking of guitar, you still haven't given me my lessons." Caroline pouted, embracing the change in topic and the lighter mood.

"My God, woman." Jax smiled down at her. "What more do you want from me?"

"No guitar lesson, no sucky-sucky," Caroline said seriously, but was trying hard not to laugh.

Jax's laugh boomed through the room as he didn't hold back. "I'll definitely be bringing my guitar tomorrow and starting those lessons."

The rest of the night they lay together talking, laughing, and finally getting to really know each other. No other thoughts of work, issues, or Mika filled her thoughts. Instead, they savored their time, not willing to face reality quite yet.

## Chapter 27

It had been three days since Jax had confessed his love for Caroline and he felt different, in a good way. True to his word, he had Blaze bring his guitar out the next day and had started lessons with Caroline. She was a fast learner, but the teacher in her had her asking so many questions that they made Jax's head swim.

The training, and search for Mika, as well as his other duties, hadn't stopped and when he was away from her, no matter who he left in charge to guard her, he wasn't at ease until he was back at her side.

Riding back to her house after a long day, he was excited to give her the gift he had bought. Pulling into the driveway, he nodded to Adam and Steve, who were finishing up the roof, along with Duncan and Damon. He grabbed her gift, hurrying to the front door.

Once inside, he found her instantly. She turned when he entered, tossed her paintbrush down, and ran to him.

"Wait!" He held his hand out, stopping her, while the other was behind his back. "I have something for you."

"For me?" She smiled, trying to look around him, but he moved so she couldn't see.

"Of course for you, who else?" He grinned, then quickly frowned. "Close your eyes."

Caroline did, clasping her hands together and putting them under her chin. "I love surprises." She bounced excitedly.

Jax laughed, pulling the gift from behind him and placing it on the floor in front of her. "Okay, open your eyes."

Her eyes sprang open, gaze settling on the object before her. As her hand went to her mouth, she dropped to her knees. "Is that a guitar?"

"No, it's a puppy." Jax raised his eyebrows in humor, looking at the guitar case. He chuckled when she shot him a glare.

She carefully opened the case. "It's beautiful." She strummed the strings without taking it out. Then she started to cry.

"Caroline." Jax knelt down. Okay, this wasn't how he'd expected this to go and he wasn't sure what in the hell to do. "It's supposed to make you happy, not make you cry."

"Happy tears." She pointed to her face, crying and laughing at the same time. "I love it. Thank you so much." She threw her arms around him.

"Roof's done." Duncan walked in, with Damon, Steve, and Adam following.

Jax and Caroline stood. "Thank you, guys, so much." Caroline wiped her face. "Please let me make you something to eat real quick. I know you have to be hungry."

"No, we're good," Duncan replied, looking down at the guitar. "Nice guitar."

"Jax got it for me." Caroline beamed. "He's been teaching me how to play."

"I can play a pretty mean set of drums," Steve said, then added at the disbelieving looks, "No, seriously. I'm not being smart-ass Steve this time. I really can play drums. Maybe we can get together sometime and play."

Before anyone could say anything, Caroline's phone rang. Walking over, she picked it up. "Hey, Rachel." She smiled, but her face quickly became concerned. "Okay, let me call Mom and Dad. Maybe she went home early. I'll call you right back."

"What's wrong?" Jax was beside her.

"Today was cheerleading tryouts but Jamie didn't show up, even though she was at school. Rachel said she was excited, so she doesn't understand why Jamie wouldn't show up." Caroline hit her parents' number, putting her phone to her ear. "Hi, Dad."

Jax glanced over at Duncan and Damon, who listened closely. Their eyes met in silent, mutual understanding. Damon pulled out his phone and walked outside.

"Did Jamie come home from school?" Caroline's worried eyes landed on Jax. She shook her head. "I know. Rachel called and said she didn't show up. What about Mom, has she heard from her? Okay, let me call Rachel back and see if she showed up yet. Maybe she just got held up in her last class."

Jax watched Caroline's hands shake as she tried to call Rachel back. "Calm down, Caroline."

Caroline nodded. "Rachel, has she shown up yet?" Caroline listened and he knew by the look on her face Jamie hadn't. "No, Mom and Dad haven't heard from her. I'm going to call Lana now. What? Who said that?"

Damon walked back inside, shaking his head at Jax.

"That doesn't make sense." Caroline bit her lip as she listened, her frown deepening. "Why would she be talking to Pete? Okay, let me call Lana. Please call me if she shows up."

"I called Sid, and Lana hasn't heard from her. They're on their way to the school now," Damon informed them.

"Who's Pete?" Jax asked. He was no longer the smiling man from moments before. He was in full Warrior mode.

"He's one of the janitors at the school." Caroline

frowned. "But in all the years I've been there, I've never seen him converse with the students, and with Jamie being a freshman, he wouldn't know her."

\*\*\*\*\*\*

The more time that went by, the more Caroline's panic heightened. A missing persons alert had been issued, even though it hadn't been twenty-four hours. Her dad and Lana had connections and used them with no problem.

Caroline sat with the phone in her hand, and she couldn't get the thought of why Pete had spoken to her sister in the parking lot out of her head. Something nagged her and she couldn't shake it. Pete had been acting strange when last she'd seen him, but maybe he was just having an off day, plus she hadn't seen him all summer. And Jamie was a smart, strong girl. Lana had taught them both self-defense moves. Pete was an older man with a limp and was slumped over. She tried to convince herself not to overthink it.

Caroline stood when Lana and Sid walked in. "Anything?"

"Yeah." Lana frowned, looking worried. "This janitor, Pete, says he didn't talk to her. He said today was his first day back to work after getting sick and leaving work Monday morning. He worked mostly in the auditorium today to get it ready for a band concert tonight."

Caroline's head snapped back. "Wait a minute." Caroline glanced at Adam and Steve. "That can't be right. I talked to Pete the day I worked. He came in my room and then again in the office. The secretary saw him, as did Jill, Steve, and Adam. Jamie was also in the office."

"If it's the same old guy, Adam about ran him over in the hallway," Steve added.

"He couldn't have been," Lana said, checking her notes. "The principal confirmed this. He also confirmed that at the time the student said she saw the janitor talking to Jamie, he was with the janitor in the auditorium, along with two other teachers who also confirmed."

"Oh, my God." Her eyes swung to Jax. "He's got my sister."

"Who's got her, Caroline?" Lana clutched her arm.

"My brother." Jax pulled Caroline to him, holding her. "He won't hurt her. He wants something and wants to make sure I know he's got her."

"He wants me," Caroline replied. "The bastard wants me in trade for my sister because he hasn't been able to get to me. This is how he's going to do it."

"He isn't going to do anything," Jax promised. "I won't let him."

"I called everyone. They're on their way." Duncan stepped in. "Keep your phone lines open because he's going to contact someone, and soon. We need to have a plan in place when he does."

Steve walked up, looking like he was ready to burst. "I've got the plan."

"Steve, please," Adam said, glancing at Caroline and Lana. "Now's not the time."

"Ah, hello... who's the dumb ass now?" Steve pointed at himself, then frowned. "I mean, guess who's not the dumb ass now? Me, that's who."

When no one said anything Steve rolled his eyes.

"How about we talk about your newly acquired power, Adam 'who reads everyone even when blocked as long as he touches them' Pride?" Steve twirled his hand, urging Adam to understand what the fuck he was saying.

"Holy shit!" Adam looked shocked, then punched Steve in excitement. "I ran into the fucker. If Mika did shift into Pete, I ran into him. Holy shit!"

Steve rubbed his shoulder. "If that's the way you say thank you, then keep it to your damn self."

"Can you get a read on him?" Jax let go of Caroline to head toward Adam.

"Hold on." Adam walked out on the porch. "Give me a minute. I need to focus."

No one said a word as they waited. Lana came over and held Caroline's hand as Jax paced, waiting for Adam.

"I got the bastard." Adam's smile wasn't pleasant.

Jax walked over, kissing Caroline hard. "I swear I'm going to get her back unharmed."

"Stay here with Caroline," Sid told Lana.

Caroline shook her head. "No, I'm fine." Caroline wanted nothing more than to go with them, but knew she would only be in the way and didn't want Jax worrying about her. Jamie was what was important. "Go, Lana. She can call backup from the police department if needed."

"I don't like leaving you here alone." Jax frowned, hesitating.

"Adam will know if he leaves," Caroline urged him. "Just get Jamie back safe. That's all that matters. He doesn't even know you guys are on to him. I'm safe."

Jax kissed her one more time. "I'll call you as soon as we have her," he assured her and turned to leave, but stopped. Looking at her over his shoulder, he said, "I love you." It was the first time he had said it to her first and her heart soared.

"I love you, too. Please be careful." Caroline watched as they took off just as the rest of the Warriors arrived. She wanted to wallow in his words of love, but she was too worried about him, about all of them. There would be time for that later. Mika was finally going to pay for all the tragedy he had caused. She just prayed her sister wasn't hurt, but she trusted Jax and knew he would get her back.

## Chapter 28

Caroline paced around her house with her phone in her hand. She was a nervous wreck and didn't know what to do with herself.

She had gotten her gun, actually put her clip in, but kept the safety on and had it within reach. A knock on her door scared her to death. Snatching the gun carefully, she clicked the safety off—she could thank Jax for yelling at her repeatedly for that—and went toward the front door.

"Who is it?" she called out, wishing she had a peephole. It was something she would ask Jax to organize for her.

"It's me." Her dad's voice was clear and calm.

Caroline clicked the safety back on and opened the door. "Dad." Caroline hugged him. "Where's Mom?"

"She went home." Her dad let her go quickly and then closed the door.

"Why didn't she come with you?" Caroline found that strange. Her mom, especially with Jamie possibly missing, would be glued to her dad's side.

"She's so upset about Jamie that she..." A strange

smile spread across her dad's face. "Ah, fuck it! I don't have time for this shit."

Confusion left Caroline wide-eyed and asking, "What?" Gasping for breath, she felt the color drain from her cheeks as her dad changed before her into a man she'd never laid eyes on before.

She raised the gun, but had no chance to switch off the safety before he took it from her, bending her wrist at an odd angle. She heard the crack before the pain overwhelmed her, radiating throughout her whole body.

"Who are you?" Caroline cried, backing away from him. It was no use, he stalked her until she was up against the kitchen counter. She held her wrist protectively against her chest.

"It doesn't matter." The man pulled out rope from under his jacket. "I'm just here for a paycheck. After all the bullshit I've had to put up with I should have asked for more. After figuring out who in the hell your dad was and shifting into him to fool you, which wasn't hard at all by the way, I had to hurry over here before the boss man called them. Seeing the Warriors leave was my cue. It was go time."

"Why are you doing this?" Caroline watched his every move, wishing she could do something to get away, but it looked hopeless.

"As I said, for a paycheck." The man seemed to be more than happy to talk about the plans that had been made. "Mika grabbed your sister. He's in the process of making a trade with the Warriors. You for her."

Caroline tried not to scream when he tied her hands behind her. The pain from her broken wrist almost made her pass out. "They won't do that," Caroline finally gritted out through clenched teeth.

"Obviously since they have already left you, they have." He chuckled with a snort. "He knew all along the Warriors would ride off to save the day thinking they had us, but in truth, we got them, or should I say *you*. He really wants you dead in a bad way."

A small flicker of hope found its way through the pain. This man had no idea that the Warriors hadn't left because of Mika's plan. No, they'd left because Adam was reading Mika and knew his exact location. She prayed that Adam was still reading him and would be clued in to what was happening with her.

Next he tied her feet and then forced her to sit in a chair he'd moved into the center of the house. He tied her to it and then left the house. He returned with gas cans and started spreading the fluid everywhere, the pungent smell making her eyes and nose burn. Fear gripped her. She opened her mind, screaming for Jax, not having a clue if it would work.

"You'll never get away with this," Caroline hissed, trying to move in the chair, but he had her tied too tightly. "The Warriors will hunt you down. Remember Jax Wheeler's name because he's the one coming after you."

The shifter started to back out of the room, pouring gas as he went. "I'll be long gone before they even realize what's happened. My job was to kill you, and that's what I'm going to do." He stopped, giving her a look. "No hard feelings."

"Please, don't do this," Caroline begged, dread filling her. He had left the door open and she could see him ignite the gas, the flames racing toward the house, come up the front steps, and then she felt a breeze. She turned and saw Alisha kneeling next to her, anguish on her face. "Help me, Alisha. Go get Lana, please."

When Alisha just bowed her head, Caroline knew it would be too late for help and began to cry for things that would never be. She was more worried about how Jax was going to feel when he found her. That Mika had once again taken someone he cared about from him.

Leaning her head back, she opened her mind as wide as she could. "Jax!" she screamed at the top of her lungs as the heat became intense, the smoke thick.

******

Everyone followed Adam. It was late, with hardly any traffic at all, and if they ran into any, they got around it any way they could. Jax prepared his mind for what was to come, as he was sure everyone else did.

Suddenly, Adam swerved his bike, skidding it to a complete stop in the middle of the road and looked directly at Jax. Everyone came to a screeching halt, bikes sliding sideways to avoid hitting each other.

"Get back to Caroline's, now!" Adam screamed, a look of horror on his face.

Jax didn't hesitate as he turned around and took off. He didn't ask questions, but the look on Adam's face told him everything he needed to know. Caroline was in danger. Half followed Adam while the other half went with Jax. They hadn't gotten very far before Adam had stopped.

The smell of fire rode on the wind as he reached streets near to Caroline's. He opened his bike up, scanning the area. Pulling into her drive, he barely had time to register the flames fiercely licking at the building, too focused on the echo of his name. It was Caroline.

Through the open door and the dancing flames, he spotted her tied to a chair. He slowed but didn't stop as he rode his bike through the burning flames and into the house, bursting through the burning wood. He jumped off his bike as soon as he was near her, letting the bike go out the other side of the house through the flaming wall.

Caroline coughed, not a racking cough like he

would have imagined. Instead, she drifted in and out of consciousness. He grabbed the rope at her wrists, giving it a snap to break her free. Her scream ripping through the building tore through him. He looked down and saw her wrist was clearly broken. He couldn't worry about that until he got her to safety. Once he had her out of the ropes, Jax picked her up, but as soon as he headed toward a spot to make a run for it, the ceiling collapsed, making escape impossible. He would be fine, but Caroline would be burned severely.

Anger and panic rode him hard as he turned, trying to find a safe way out for Caroline, but they were trapped. He turned again, this time seeing Blaze walking through the flames, as if there were a shield around him. The flames leaped away from him, clearing a path.

"Give me Caroline," Blaze ordered, taking her quickly.

Jax wanted to refuse. She was his responsibility, but knew his actions would cost her life. He watched as the same shield that surrounded Blaze encircled Caroline, and he wanted to drop to his knees with relief. Blaze headed through the flames with Caroline. Jax followed closely, his eyes never leaving her. He didn't care that his skin sizzled; he would be healed within minutes.

Fire trucks had pulled in and were getting set up to tackle the fire. Blaze bypassed the group of working firefighters and then carefully handed Caroline to

Jax.

"Thank you." Jax had never been more relieved to have another in his arms until that moment. He'd almost lost her.

Blaze nodded, his concerned eyes still on Caroline, who was coughing and choking nonstop. "She needs oxygen."

Slade was already directing the medics their way. He hurried toward them. "Get her in the ambulance so they can start oxygen on her."

Jax did, laying her on the stretcher carefully. Slade got in beside her, taking over and positioning the oxygen mask on her. Jax wanted nothing more than to pull her away and hold her, but he stopped himself, getting his protectiveness under control.

"Her right wrist is broken," Jax informed him. His voice hitched with anger and fear.

"Is she burned anywhere that you know of?" Slade asked as he looked at her eyes, then adjusted the oxygen.

"No, I don't think so," Jax replied, his eyes not leaving her pale face. "Is she going to be okay?"

"I won't let her be any other way," Slade promised.

Jax stayed out of the way, but close enough to touch

her. The horror of seeing her inside her burning house had terrified him. He would have burned alive to keep her safe and had felt so helpless until Blaze had stepped in. He could never repay the Warrior for what he'd done tonight.

She began coughing again, but not as bad. Slade once more adjusted the oxygen as the medics stood back, watching. Slade obviously didn't care he had taken over their jobs and Jax was glad he had. He trusted no one other than Slade with her life.

Jax took his eyes away from her long enough to look at her house. It was almost completely burned to the ground. Next to the building, he spotted four gas cans and his rage knew no bounds.

"My sister?" Caroline's voice reached him through his rage.

"They're going after her," Jax promised. He then glanced at his phone. No messages yet. "Are you okay?"

She nodded, her eyes looking past him to her house. "My guitar," she whispered, but loud enough for Jax to hear. Tears streaked her dirty face. "My house. No, not my house."

Jax tried to block her view of the fire, but he couldn't conceal the flames leaping at the darkening twilight sky.

"It wasn't Mika." Caroline pulled the mask off her

face, her voice low and raspy from smoke inhalation. "Someone knocked on the door. I asked who it was and it was my dad, or I thought it was my dad." Caroline began coughing again.

"Caroline, you need to stop talking and keep the mask on your face," Slade ordered with a worried frown.

Caroline pulled it off again. "Mika wanted you away from me so he could kill me and it didn't matter who did it. He paid someone to do it."

Jax vowed then and there that whoever else was involved in putting Caroline in danger would be hunted by him personally. He carefully put the mask back on her face. "We'll talk about that later."

Jill came up to the ambulance and leaned in toward Jax, whispering, "They have Jamie and she's uninjured." Jill looked toward Caroline, then back to Jax. "They also have Mika."

"Where?" Jax growled, keeping his voice low. He didn't want Caroline upset.

"They just pulled in," Jill replied, then jumped out of the way as Jax quickly exited the ambulance.

His eyes searched for and found the van, knowing Mika was inside. Before he reached it, Sloan stepped in front of him. "Is Caroline okay?" His worried voice broke through to Jax, but his eyes stayed zeroed in on the van.

"Slade is working on her now, but yeah, she's going to be okay," Jax finally answered, his voice sounding inhuman.

"I'm not letting you anywhere near that van. We need answers from him." Sloan's voice hardened. "And there are too many human police around to do what needs to be done with your brother. We only stopped to offer you backup since we didn't know what the fuck was going on."

Jax knew what Sloan said was true, but to let Mika leave alive when he was right there within his grasp was almost too much for him to handle. His mind and body demanded it be settled immediately by killing the son of a bitch. The sound of Caroline coughing urged those feelings, but something else also came over him. She was what was important at that very moment and he needed to be by her side.

"You will have your day with him, Jax. No one touched him other than restraining him. He's yours to deal with." Sloan put his hand on his shoulder. "Trust me on that. No one will touch him. You have my promise."

Torn between knowing what he wanted to do and what he needed to do was a war that raged inside him. Sloan may think he could stop him, but he'd have a fight on his hands. Then he heard his name. It was Caroline calling him.

"Go." Sloan nodded toward the ambulance. "Take care of her so your mind is right when you take care of your brother."

Jax's black eyes shifted from the van, where he knew Mika sat, to Sloan, who watched him closely. With a growl, he nodded, then turned and walked away. It was one of the hardest things he had ever done.

Jax got back in the ambulance and looked down at Caroline. With a shaking hand, she touched his cheek. "I heard Jill. Go, Jax," she said, this time without removing the mask. "I'm fine."

There it was. Her permission to go, take care of his brother. He knew the van hadn't left yet. Knew his brother was only a few feet away, but yet he stared into her bloodshot eyes and knew without a doubt that his life had just changed in that instant.

"I'm not going anywhere," Jax replied, kissing the palm of her hand. His priority lay before him, injured. At that exact moment, he knew the devil himself couldn't pull him away from her.

## Chapter 29

Jax sat in the waiting room waiting for Slade. It was determined that Caroline had to have surgery on her wrist. He had offered to give her his blood for healing, but Slade was afraid the break was too complex and wouldn't heal correctly.

Her parents, and Jamie, along with Lana, Sid, Jill, and Steve also waited. Slade entered the waiting room. "She did great." Relief filtered through Jax, calming his pounding blood and the knot in his stomach. "She's already been in recovery and has been placed in a private room. She needs a couple of days with oxygen so she's going to have to stay."

"Her wrist?" Jax closed his eyes at the news, embracing the welcome reprieve on his nerves.

"The surgery went extremely well and it should heal with no problems." Slade focused on Jax. "She wants to see you, Jax. Then she wants to see everyone."

Jax followed Slade to the room, barely able to restrain himself from rushing in. Caroline lay with the oxygen mask going full blast. Her face remained pale. She was hooked up to monitors and IVs, and as much as he absolutely hated seeing her like this, he was so relieved that she was breathing.

"Hey." Her voice was weak and hoarse.

Jax walked next to the bed and carefully placed a kiss to her forehead. "How you feeling?"

"Actually, pretty darn good." Caroline smiled with a chuckle, making her muffled voice more difficult to understand. "They pumped some pain meds in me and I'm liking it… a lot."

Jax laughed, brushing her hair off her face. His laughter died. "I'm sorry, Caroline."

"You hush," Caroline scolded him. She tried to remove her mask so she could speak more clearly, but he prevented her. Undeterred, she continued, "You've nothing to be sorry for. Now I'm probably going to sleep the rest of the day. I'm fine, Jax, but I need you to do something for me."

"Anything." Jax leaned down to hear her, her voice growing so low.

Her eyes opened wide and looked totally clear. "I want you to go take care of your business with Mika." When he started to say something, she hushed him again. "I want this over as I know you do. Do it, Jax. I want a life with you. With Mika still in the background, I don't feel that's possible. Do what you have to do, what needs to be done. If you don't…"

"If I don't?" Jax frowned.

"No sucky-sucky for you." She barked out a laugh at the shocked look on his face. "Sorry, it's the pain meds talking."

"Sure it is." He chuckled.

"Seriously, Jax." Caroline again opened her eyes to stare at him. "I love you, but you need to take care of this and then come back to me. Now, go and send in the rest of the crew so they can make fun of me while I'm on these pain meds, but please don't let them post any videos on Facebook or YouTube. "

Jax carefully kissed her on the lips. "I love you." For such a long time he couldn't even say those three words, now he couldn't stop staying them. That single moment in the ambulance when she urged him to leave her to take care of his brother told him everything he needed to know. She understood him and accepted him for who and what he was. Yet, even with her blessing of letting him go, he couldn't leave her until he knew she was going to be okay.

"Just promise to come back to me." Caroline whispered her eyes fighting to stay open. "Please come back to me."

"I'll always come back to you, Caroline." Jax leaned over and kissed her forehead. She had already dozed off so he stood, staring at her for a few minutes before turning and leaving the room. Emotion so powerful flooded through him, ready to choke him. He went to the waiting room to send in everyone else, but stopped Slade.

"Can I borrow your car?" Jax glanced between Slade

and Jill.

"You good, or do you need me to drive you?" Jill asked helpfully.

"I'm good, thanks." He quickly replied, remembering the driving lessons he gave her. Yeah, he was good. He turned, walking away. "I'll bring it back soon."

"We'll meet you there," Slade called out, the hidden meaning behind those words plain to Jax.

******

After leaving the hospital, Jax went directly to Sloan's office. After being briefed about everything that had happened from the point of them finding Jamie to his incarceration, Jax anxiously left Sloan's office and headed straight toward the interrogation room where Mika had been kept as uncomfortably as possible. He nodded at Damon, who stood guard outside the room, then opened the door. He knew the rest of the Warriors were nearby for what was to come.

He walked in, observing Mika sitting at the table, chained to a chair.

"Hey, brother." Mika grinned. "Heard the little cunt made it out of the fire. Way to go, hero."

Forcing his face to remain impassive, Jax walked over and punched Mika in the mouth. Feeling slightly less ready to rip Mika apart that second, he pulled out a chair and sat down.

"Okay, that hurt a little bit." Mika spat blood, then ran his tongue along his teeth.

"Who did you hire to set the fire?" Jax asked, his tone level, without even a hint of hate edging his voice. He was past hating his brother.

"Fuck you!" his brother spat, but instead of blood, his hatred spewed forth.

Jax reacted quickly, punching Mika in the throat. "Wrong answer."

Once Mika was able to talk, which he had to try to do three times, he continued to be a bastard. "You know this has nothing to do with the bitch or her sister." Mika rolled his head back and forth. Pausing, his gaze zeroed in on Jax, his eyes filled with contempt.

"Who did you hire to set the fire?" Jax repeated, not falling for his goading.

"My goal has been and will always be to see you suffer," Mika sneered. "I want you to live forever and watch every person in your life die knowing it was your fault. Just like Alisha, who died because of you."

"Send Adam in," Jax called, his eyes never leaving Mika.

"You were always pathetic," Mika hissed in agitation that Jax wasn't taking the bait. "Father didn't want to banish me, but because of you, he had no choice."

Jax ignored him, knowing it was a lie that he wouldn't fall for, and waited for Adam. He was not playing Mika's games.

Adam walked in, closing the door behind him. He stared at Mika without saying a word. "The guy's name is Tarvin McMann."

"Pretty impressive." Mika stared at Adam. "Tell him what I'm thinking now."

Adam laughed, then looked at Jax. "Please tell me you're going to kill this son of a bitch and soon."

Jax didn't respond, just stared at Mika.

"Oh, and Tarvin drives a black Ford Ranger. He's supposed to meet up with this asshole tomorrow at the bus station for his money at… 6:00 p.m. He was going to stand him up anyway." Adam gave him an evil grin. "The harder you try to block, the easier you are to read… fucker. And yeah, I'm the one who fucked up your plans."

"Oh, I have many more plans," Mika spat toward Adam. "You young fuck. Just wait, I'll make you suffer right along with this piece of shit."

"Thanks, Adam," Jax dismissed Adam. He had

every intention of being there to meet the fucker, Tarvin. For now, his main focus was on Mika.

"No problem." Adam gave Mika a knowing grin as he left the room.

"Guess that's all I need from you." Jax stood and started to remove the silver chains holding him to the chair.

"Oh, great." Mika stretched. "Where to now?"

"Hell," Jax responded, stepping away to give him room to walk by. The flash of fear in Mika's eyes gave Jax some satisfaction, but not enough.

Sloan opened the door, pulling Mika out of the room. Sloan and Duncan were on each side, with Damon in front and Jax behind. They headed into another room where Damon hit a button on the wall. The wall slid open, exposing a hidden elevator. The men stepped inside. Damon hit the down button and the door closed.

"What, no music?" Mika responded. His fear couldn't be disguised by his bravado. It filled the elevator, sending a spark of satisfaction through Jax.

The doors opened into a large room. Slade, Jill, Steve, Jared, Adam, Blaze, and Sid were all present. Sloan and Duncan shepherded Mika to the middle of the room and then moved away. Jax walked up and stood in front of him.

"What is this?" Mika looked around, his gaze once more landing on Jax.

"You and I are going to settle this once and for all." Jax looked toward the Warriors. He'd made a promise to Caroline that it would be finished today. She had been right. With Mika, there was no future for them and today, that would change, one way or another. "I don't care what happens. I do not want anyone stepping in. What will be… will be."

Each Warrior gave a nod of acceptance, but didn't say a word—well, except for Jared.

"You hear that?" Jared glanced at Damon. "No decapitations."

"We'll see," Damon responded, still staring straight ahead.

"You against me?" Mika laughed nervously. "I've beaten you at everything."

Jax took off his shirt, tossing it aside. "We've never paired up in a fair fight. Today we will and you will lose." Jax took a step forward. "Each name inked on my skin is a person you killed. Today, each will get their revenge from your flesh."

"Oh, you want to play that way?" Mika tilted his head. "Okay, I'll play."

Everyone watched as Mika shifted into an older Indian man. "Son, you failed us."

"Your games won't work." Jax cut him off before he could say anything more. Instead, he moved into his space and punched Mika in the face. The contact forced Mika to shift back. "So step up and fight like a man." Jax shoved him across the room.

Mika's roar echoed as he charged Jax, but Jax stepped completely out of the way, punching Mika in the back of the head as he passed. Mika turned, his face flamed with rage.

"Who you going to turn into next?" Jax cracked his neck back and forth. "How about Alisha? Go ahead, Mika, shift. You owe her flesh and I'll be happy to collect on her behalf."

This time when Mika rushed him, Jax took the hit, then flipped his brother over in a body slam, landing on top of him. Jax pressed the heel of his hand against Mika's throat to push himself up.

"Seems without your tricks, you're just a little pussy. Without your band of renegades to slaughter innocents, you are nothing," Jax hissed, then spat on him. "You are nothing, Mika. Get up and face me."

Weapons decorated the room and Mika spotted them. He crawled to a knife and grabbed it. Jax allowed him to take it, unconcerned by the coward before him. Mika stood and rushed toward Jax, slashing wildly. Jax took a slash on the arm as he used both hands on each side of Mika's wrist to dislodge the knife from his grip. Jax caught the knife in midair, flipped it, grasped the handle and buried it in Mika's shoulder. "That was for Alisha, you son of a bitch."

Mika's scream of pain reverberated around the room. Jax had slammed it down so hard that part of the handle was buried in his shoulder.

"Here, let me help you." Jax knocked Mika's hands away from the knife, put his foot on his crotch, and pushed with his foot as he yanked the knife out, making sure that it moved as much as possible. Jax tossed the knife away. "You want to try the sword next?"

"That's it." Mika dropped to his knees. "I give."

Unmoved by Mika's pathetic attempt for leniency, Jax's laugh was bitter. "Did you give mercy to the innocent women and children who you murdered, or the elders who you scalped?" When Mika remained silent, Jax grabbed him by his throat, lifting him to face him. "No, you didn't. So I will show no mercy to you. I could have killed you outright and no one here would have said a word, but I'm giving you a chance to win the fair way. That's why you will lose. You don't know the fair way."

Mika's hard stare was filled with hatred. "I enjoyed killing every one of those traitors. None of them stood up for me," Mika wheezed. "I would do it all over again if I had the chance. And as for Alisha, she only loved you. She hated me. I hope the bitch burns in hell."

Powerful fists met warm flesh as Jax unleashed his pain as well as justice on Mika. The bastard had been in this world long enough. When Mika was close to passing out, Jax forced him on his knees as he grabbed a hand full of hair tilting his brothers head back so he had to stare up at him. Reaching behind him with his free hand, he removed the knife he always carried.

"Many of our people went to meet death in shame because of your disrespect." Jax gripped the knife handle tightly. "It is time for fate to claim you in death, but I am your reaper."

"You would do this to your own brother?" Mika stared up at him, his mouth set in a hateful sneer.

"You are no brother to me." Jax replied evenly. The sound of chanting echoed in his head and for a slight moment, he wondered if it was his ancestors giving their blessing on what he was about to do, but his eye rose from Mika. The Warriors watched, their voices in time with each other as they chanted in the old language, their fists slamming against their chests. They were his true brothers.

Jax began a chant of his own, loud enough that Mika heard him. It was the death chant of their ancestors. For just this moment, he was not a VC Warrior, but a Native American from old. Lifting the knife, he yanked hard on Mika's scalp with his other hand as the knife slid across Mika's skin like butter. Yeah, he kept his knife that sharp.

Within seconds, Jax lifted Mika's severed scalp, throwing his own head back and screamed a war-cry that had everyone go silent. Looking back down at Mika, he threw the scalp at him before stepping back. The bloody scalp fell at Mika's knees. "That was for every person you dishonored in *my* tribe."

Knowing that wouldn't kill Mika, he waited for Mika to stop his moaning and screaming, which he finally did. He managed to stand and face Jax. He looked grotesque without his scalp with blood streaking down his face.

"Any last words before death comes to collect you?" Jax said, his voice void of any emotion. Jax looked away from him, not even afraid of Mika making a move and wished he would, and looked to Sloan who threw him a sword which he caught easily.

"I spit on the names you wear on your skin." Mika's eyes narrowed as he cursed his insult. Before he could spit on Jax, Jax brought the sword up, spun in the air and, as he came down, the sword sliced through Mika's neck, severing his head.

"That was for me, motherfucker." Jax stared down at his brother. Tossing the sword on his dead body, he glanced at Sloan. "I'm going to the hospital if anyone needs me."

"Damn, dude." Sid looked over at Damon. "I think a new badass has been crowned. Scalping *and* decapitation, I mean holy fucking shit!"

"Shut up, asshole." Damon grumbled, this there was respect as he looked at Jax.

Jax heard Sid, but didn't say a word as he picked up his shirt and stepped on the elevator without turning around. When the door closed, Jax slumped, his body trembling, his relief was so great and yet he had no remorse. He felt a sense of freedom he hadn't felt in a long time. When he knew the door would be opening, he stood straight and proud, cracking his neck back and forth. Just another day in the office.

## Chapter 30

Caroline had been anxious to get out of the hospital. After inhaling more smoke than anyone realized, she'd been forced to stay a total of six days. Slade refused her discharge until her lungs were clear. A course of oxygen, as well as breathing treatments, finally seemed to have worked, which meant she was home free.

"Where are we going?" Caroline looked over at Jax, then out the car window.

"You'll see." He smiled without looking at her. "Just sit back and enjoy being out of the hospital."

Caroline sighed with a smile. The night he'd returned to her, he came back a changed man. All he'd said was that Mika would never bother them again. He'd then crawled into her hospital bed and held her the rest of the night. The nurses weren't too happy about that, but Jax didn't care and neither had she. Caroline never asked any questions about that night and she never would. If Jax wanted to talk about it, she would listen.

Lana had told her that they'd found the man who had set her house on fire with her in it, but that was all she knew. The only thing Sid would tell her was that he had been dealt with and would never be a bother to them again. Caroline wondered if there was something behind the phrase "'never be a bother to them again.'" She also had only seen Alisha once since the night of the fire. She had come to say good-bye. Caroline really hoped that Alisha finally found peace.

Jax reached over and grabbed her uninjured hand in his. "You still taking the pain medicine?"

"No, why?" Caroline gave him a sideways look.

"No reason, just wondering." He turned his head and she knew he was grinning.

"I swear you and my family are awful." Caroline gave his hand a sharp tug. "I react weird and can't help what I say on that stuff."

"You're hilarious." Jax lifted her hand, leaned over and kissed it.

"You guys just like to make fun of me, that's all." Caroline couldn't help but laugh. "What did I say to Slade? No one will tell me and now every time I see him, he seems uncomfortable."

"You asked him repeatedly if he was sure he wasn't a gynecologist. When he said no, you asked him if he wanted to be and you'd be his first patient." Jax gave her a fake frown. "I kind of wanted to kill him, but then I realized it was the meds talking."

"Oh, my God." Caroline banged her head on the window. "You're lying, I didn't really do that."

"Yeah, babe, you did." Jax nodded, still grinning.

"I bet Jill hates me." Caroline cringed, her cheeks heating.

"No, she was actually laughing her ass off and teasing Slade unmercifully," Jax replied, pulling into her driveway.

"What are we doing here?" Caroline sat up, her eyes taking in everything. "What's going on?"

Jax pulled up and parked. Getting out, he went around to open her door. Caroline stepped out. Her old house was totally gone. Nothing was left but the old barn. Heavy equipment was moving dirt around as men placed markers.

"They're getting the area ready to build our new house." Jax put his arm around her, leading her toward a trailer that was parked away from where the house was being built. "The builder is just waiting for us to tell them what we want, and they're ready to start."

"You're building me a house?" Caroline felt the tears well up.

"No, we are building *us* a house." Jax leaned down, kissing her on the temple. "Now come on. We need to go over some plans so they can start, and then we have things to catch up on."

"What kind of things, Jax Wheeler?" Caroline

smiled up at him.

"Well, for one, you becoming my mate." Jax looked into the distance as he spoke.

"What?" Caroline tugged on his hair to make him look at her.

"Will you be my mate, Caroline Fitzpatrick?" Jax had never sounded more sincere than he did at that moment.

"I would love nothing more than to be your mate, Jax." Caroline couldn't hold it in any longer, the tears came. She didn't care who was there or who was watching. She clung to him and kissed him like a starved woman, a happy woman who was finally getting what she wanted most, and that was Jax Wheeler.

"If we don't stop, we will never go in that trailer because I will take you home now." Jax growled down at her.

"Take me home, Jax." Caroline rested her head on his chest, her heart beating erratically. "That's the only thing I want to do right now. I want to become your mate before we do anything else."

Jax didn't argue. He led her to the truck, but Caroline stopped and turned, confusion dipping her brows. "Wait a minute." She looked back toward where her house used to stand, then to Jax. "Where exactly is home?"

"I've got it covered." Jax smiled, helping her into the car. "Trust me."

"Always." She smiled up at him, excited for their new start, and it was a new start for them. She had never asked what happened with Mika; she didn't care. The difference in Jax was incredible. He seemed happy and that was all she cared about.

As they drove away, Alisha watched them go with a smile on her face. She looked around, then up to the sky, and with a nod she began to fade.

******

Sloan wanted to just toss his whole desk out the window. "Fuck." He shuffled papers, but couldn't find what he was looking for. "Dammit…. Shit."

The knock on the door made him cringe, count to ten, and curse. "What?"

Jill peeked in. "Hey."

"Please do not beat around the fucking bush by saying hey." Sloan growled, his eyes narrowing on her. "Spit it out or get out."

"You remember when we had those interviews…?" Jill stopped speaking at Sloan's glare. "I mean, of course you remember. Well, you told Caroline that you would interview her friend."

"No, I did not." Sloan emphasized each word with a growl. If he were a smart man, he would beg Jill to get someone in there and pronto. He was busier than fuck and with the shifters getting crazy and trying to form their own council, he was drowning, but dammit, he didn't want anyone trying to help him.

"Uh, actually, you did... twice," Jill replied. "That day you... well, you didn't say anything so she took it as you saying yes. And then at the hospital, you said yes, which I heard."

"Me saying nothing at all does not mean yes." Sloan slammed his hand on his desk. "And at the hospital, she was so drugged up I seriously doubt she remembers that."

"Yeah, well about that... she does... remember." Jill looked everywhere in the room other than at Sloan. "She set up an interview for you."

"Well, cancel it." Sloan was not in a good mood and it was getting worse by the minute.

"It's a little late." Jill actually took two steps back. "She's here."

"You have got to be fucking kidding me." Sloan's eyes started to glow black.

"Um, nope... I'm not." Jill cringed, waiting for Sloan to blow.

"This is it!" Sloan pointed at her. "After this, no

women other than the women who are already grandfathered in—"

"Grandfathered in?" Jill frowned.

"Yes, grandfathered in, meaning if you are already here, you're okay until you give me a reason to kick your bony ass out, which in your case is three strikes. And you are so close to that third strike." Sloan dropped his hand.

Jill just stared at him and he stared at her. "Uh, okay, are you going to finish?"

Sloan honestly forgot what the hell his point was, but he'd be damned if he let her know that. "Jill, let the damn woman in so she can get the hell out."

"Oh, yes, sir." Jill quickly headed for the door. "I really think you're going to like her."

"Jill!" Sloan warned, his patience very thin.

"Okay, okay." Jill frowned and opened the door. "You can come in now."

Sloan watched as the redhead he remembered from the day of hell Jill created walked in his office. He stood.

"Hi, Mr. Murphy." She stuck out her hand. "I'm Becky Spencer. I don't know if you remember me."

Sloan took her hand, careful not to hurt her as he shook it. "Nice to meet you, Ms. Spencer. Please have a seat." He left out whether he remembered her or not. He didn't have time for this shit. Even though she was damn well better looking than his Warriors that filled his office daily, he didn't want someone underfoot. It was his office, dammit. Before he could say he wasn't interested in a secretary, his phone rang. "I'm sorry, but I have to take this."

The woman nodded, her eyes never wavering from his.

"Yeah," he answered, and a frown quickly followed. "No, I haven't found it yet. I have nothing with a letterhead that looks like a skyline." Sloan rummaged around his desk again.

The woman reached out, grabbed a piece of paper, and held it up. "Is this what you're looking for?"

Surprise widened Sloan's eyes as he nodded and took it from her. "Yeah, just found it." Sloan glanced over at Jill, who gave him a thumbs-up. At his glare, she hurried out the door, closing it behind her. "I'm going to have to call you back, Gary."

Hanging up, he stared at the paper he had been searching for for over an hour, amazed that she had found it in three seconds flat.

"So, about that job." Becky gave him a bright smile.

# AUTHOR NOTE

Yes, Sloan's book is going to be next. No, this will NOT be the last book in the series. I have listened to you all and have decided to change my mind. You want Sloan and I feel Sloan is ready to be told.

The great thing about being an indie author and a woman is I can change my mind. HA! Thank you so much for having such powerful feelings about this series and know that I hear every single one of you who reach out. Because of you Sloan gets his story next and yes, he is grumbling about it. Oh, the things to be told.....

## COMING SOON

'Lee County Wolves' Book #2

'The Protectors Series' Book #9 Sloan

Find out more about me and the Warriors at

www.teresagabelman.com

https://www.facebook.com/pages/Teresa-Gabelman/191553587598342?ref=bookmarks

Printed in Great Britain
by Amazon